MIND HACK

A Cyberpunk Saga
Book 4
MATTHEW A. GOODWIN

Independently published

Copyright© 2021 Matthew Goodwin

ISBN Number 978-1-7340692-2-8

Editor: Joanne Paulson

Cover design by Christian Bentulan

MIND HACK

A CYBERPUNK SAGA

BOOK 4

MATTHEW A. GOODWIN

This is one is for you, mom.

PART I

CHAPTER 1

Moss couldn't help but smile as he appraised the party on the rooftop garden. People, young and old, were milling about, having drinks, eating freshly prepared meals and chatting about their lives. All former employees of ThutoCo and residents of the burbs, they were now free citizens who could choose how to spend their time and money for themselves.

The high-rise apartment complex had been rented exclusively to any employee who jumped ship after Moss had exposed ThutoCo's wrongdoings. Lanterns swung gently in the breeze, strung between tall meta pillars. Dueling barbecues filled the air with smoke scented of real meats, fruits and vegetables. Kids splashed in an infinity pool whose edge appeared to drop off to BA City below. Office workers forced to stay late in nearby buildings gawked at the reverie.

Moss marveled at how much some things had changed. He had been gone for some time and had been so focused on what was before him that he had no time to ponder if his actions made any impact.

They had.

He made his way through the crowd to where Steampuck, an ally Moss had saved from certain death in Africa, was looking over the city. He wore the Victorian era garb he so loved with an antique blunderbuss slung on a leather strap over his shoulder. His mustache was trimmed and perfectly waxed, and he stood with a proud posture.

"Evening," Moss said, breaking the man's attention from his thoughts. "Quite a view."

"It is that," Puck said, a slight smile curling under his thick mustache. He turned to look back at all the bright lights of buildings and advertisements in the dark. "I'm reminded of what Jugurtha said when appraising Roma Antiqua: urbem venalem et mature perituram, si emptorem invenerit."

Moss shook his head. "I've just spent the last month there, chasing down Judy in a virtual reality game that took place in Ancient Rome. If I never hear about Roma Antiqua again, it'll be too soon."

Puck scoffed and remained silent.

"Fine, what does it mean?" Moss allowed, in too good a mood to be bothered.

"A city for sale and doomed to quick destruction, if it should find a buyer," Puck intoned. Moss noticed Puck gave the look he always did when he found himself to be immensely clever.

"That's apt, but I've got news for you," Moss said.

Puck smirked. "It already has found a buyer."

"Exactly." Moss tapped his finger to his nose.

"Hence the good fight," Puck said, lifting his glass.

Moss clinked his glass against Puck's. They smiled and Puck looked once more into the city. From the top of the midlevel building, opulence stretched above them with destitution below.

"Since doing away with Alice Carcer in Africa, the Carcer Corporation does seem to have doubled its efforts here," Puck said, almost absentmindedly.

Moss nodded. "Yeah, we hit the hornet's nest with that one."

"Worry you?" Puck asked.

Moss shook his head. "The other crews are running interference to give us some space to work. They know we have shit that needs doing."

"Kindness through chaos," Puck observed.

"Right," Moss said, taking a sip and following Puck's gaze out into the city. After a moment, he asked, "You doing all right?"

"I am a stranger in a strange land, yet most is much the same," Puck said evasively.

"I meant," Moss began, but Puck cut him off.

"I know what you were asking," he said, falling silent. They had spoken a few times about his sister's death but Moss's guilt over the situation constantly made him want to ask.

"I'm doing as well as can be expected, given the circumstances. Irene was an amazing person and a guiding light through the dark. Better it was her standing here than I, but such is life," he said in a measured tone and raised his glass to the sky before taking another sip.

Moss did the same and Puck turned to look him right in the eyes. "Moss," his voice quavered. "There is one thing which I have never said to you that I must."

Moss held up his hands. "No, there's no need."

"I must," Puck repeated. "Thank you. I had descended into a madness of loss and despite myself, you pulled me out. It is a noble thing," Puck said, his eyes wet. "Irene," he whispered, voice breaking. "She would have been proud."

Moss felt a deep sadness well within him. "Thank you for saying that and I'm happy you are with us."

"I am as well," Puck agreed with a hint of something Moss could not quite put his finger on. "Though my antiquated ways are often at odds with your own."

"Maybe, but it's a help," Moss told him. "More often than not, we need a different way of looking at things, approaching situations. For someone who loves to tout their abilities, I think deep down, you underestimate yourself."

They both turned as a piano which had sat empty all evening now resonated through the night.

"She used to say the same thing," Puck smiled sadly. "The Moonlight Sonata, how fitting," he said as Moss listened to the somber notes.

The crowd parted just enough for Moss to see an older man sitting at the keyboard, his orange hair slicked back. Draped over his shoulder was Mr. Greene, Moss's former boss at ThutoCo and the man who had been instrumental in breaking Moss's grandmother out of Carcer City. He was dressed like a businessman after work, wearing gray slacks with a tucked in button-up blue shirt and no tie.

His heart nearly leapt from his chest at the sight. He excused himself from Puck and made his way quickly through the bodies.

"Mr. Greene!" he cried as he pulled the man to him.

As they embraced, Mr. Greene said, "I told you that you could call me Thomas."

Moss smiled. "And I told you that I didn't think I could."

"It's so wonderful to see you," he said, and Moss simply continued to smile. He couldn't help but notice that his old mentor appeared to have aged years in the months they had been apart. Dark bags hung under his eyes and wrinkles had invaded his face. He turned Moss by the shoulders. "This is my husband, Brian."

The man at the piano did not look up until he struck the last note to scattered applause. He stood, straightened his jacket, moved the chair under the piano and turned with a hand extended.

"A pleasure," he said.

"It's great to finally meet you," Moss told him sincerely.

When Moss returned from Africa, he had heard that Mr. Greene was out looking for Brian but hadn't heard anything else about him since. Not until recently. Moss had been terrified that the two would find themselves back in Carcer City or killed by ThutoCo, so it was an immense relief to see them together now.

"I must say," Brian said, looking Moss over, "I expected you to be bigger."

Moss snorted a laugh as Mr. Greene slapped Brian playfully on the shoulder.

"Brian!" Mr. Greene scolded.

"My apologies," Brian said. "I just mean that your presence looms so large, I'm surprised you're so slight."

Moss chuckled. "I'll try to be bigger next time."

"If you could," Brian smiled.

"So," Moss said, getting to the meat of it. "Was it you guys who put this all together?"

Brian averted his eyes sheepishly as Mr. Greene put a hand on his husband's shoulder. "More him than me, but we did help to make this happen."

"How?" Moss asked. "My grandmother has told me so little, and I've been occupied recently—stuck in the Mass Illusion VR."

"Ah," Mr. Greene said, squeezing Brian's shoulder.

Brian looked up from the ground at Moss. "Well, you see, your actions set many dominos tumbling. ThutoCo's perceived loss of power caused many other players to act. Most of those are simply smaller self-interested parties, but others can be potential allies if given the right direction. We provided that direction."

"Can they be trusted?" Moss asked dubiously.

Mr. Greene laughed. "Almost certainly not, but they are a means to an end."

"Persimmon LeBeau, the person who donated this building and keeps it off the company's radar, is running for mayor this year and hopes to use actions like this to garner votes from the disenfranchised. Since the major companies currently own the government, we hope to use this candidate as a weapon against their complete dominance," Brian explained.

Moss furrowed his brows. "Can they win?"

"Probably not," Mr. Greene said. "But hopefully we can weaken the corporate stranglehold on the city."

"Much like Julius Caesar in Gaul," Brian put in.

Moss groaned. "Seriously?" Exhaustion with the subject was clear in his tone even though he knew the two men didn't understand why.

"Yes," Mr. Greene said, his face lighting up. He always enjoyed a good lecture. "When Caesar invaded Gaul, he backed the smaller factions which were at war with the larger. By doing so, he ensured the destruction of the smaller as well as a weakening of the larger before taking them on headlong."

"Did you all take a class together or something?" Moss joked more to himself than to them. When he was met with nothing but blank stares, he added, "But I see your point."

"Good," Brian approved.

"We have many irons in the fire while you forge ahead with . . . " here Mr. Greene paused. "What is it that you are working on?"

Moss glanced around to ensure no one was listening and upward to confirm that the drones overhead were theirs. "We acquired some Carcer technology, but we need Judy to take a look at it. I'm meeting with them tomorrow."

"Judy is more than one person?" Brian asked and Mr. Greene audibly gasped.

"No," Moss told him. "They prefer that pronoun."

Brian winced at his foolishness. "Oh, my, yes, of course."

"We have a lot of moving parts but I'm happy to hear that things are moving in the right direction," Moss said by way of changing the subject.

"My sources within ThutoCo tell me that they are bracing for a war with Carcer," Brian added.

Moss nodded and took a sip of his drink. "I've heard the same. Better for us if they are focused on fighting each other."

"Truly," Mr. Greene said. He looked around the party. "I've seen your friend Gibbs but not Izzy. You three were practically joined at the hip in your workdays. Will she be joining us this evening?"

Moss grimaced. He had been desperate to see Izzy when he returned to B.A. City from Africa. Things had been strained between them since he had shot her when he believed she betrayed him. He had needed to see her so that he could sort out his feelings but when he called, he found out that she was in Seattle visiting a sick aunt.

They had chatted over holovid but it just wasn't the same. Their conversations continued to feel strained and Moss was heartbroken.

"My apologies," Mr. Greene said, reading Moss's face.

"It's okay," Moss said quietly. "Life is nothing if not complicated."

"We should be grateful for those types of complications now, given everything," Mr. Greene said as a playful smile crossed his lips.

"What?" Moss asked, inadvertently smiling too.

Brian and Mr. Greene exchanged glances. For two men Moss took to be in their forties, they looked like giddy children.

"What?" Moss asked again, though he had a guess.

"We are adopting!" Mr. Greene finally exclaimed.

"That's wonderful!" Moss nearly shouted and grabbed the two for another hug. He could tell that Brian was not enthusiastic about being grabbed by a near stranger, but Moss didn't care. "I'm really happy for you both."

"Thank you," they said in unison.

"So, adoption?" Moss asked, knowing that they had been saving up to design a baby all their own.

"Another impact you've had on us," Brian said with a coy smile.

Moss was confused. "*I've* had?"

"Well, yes, you and the others," Mr. Greene told him. "We came to realize that there are so many children in this city who need good homes and loving parents. Back in the burbs, we were blind to the reality of the world. But now, being out and seeing the pervasive poverty, we wanted to make an impact not just for ourselves, but for the community at large."

"We would never have known if not for you," Brian added.

Moss blushed. "That's great," he said, before adding, "It's hard to know sometimes. Know if you're making a difference, I mean. Know if anything you're doing is having an effect."

"It is," Mr. Greene assured him. "On both a macro and micro scale."

Moss smiled, truly happy for them. They continued to chat idly for a while before Moss caught sight of his grandmother standing at a spot on the roof she loved. There was a gap in the railing where a maintenance crew had removed a rusting piece but not replaced it. She had told him it was one of her favorite places —standing precariously at the edge of the building, feeling like it was the edge of the world.

"If you'll excuse me," Moss told the men. "And congratulations again."

They smiled and nodded as he walked away. Sandra was not dressed for a party but, as she always was these days, ready for battle. She wore a long leather duster that was black but turning white from wear at the folds and from pockets full of weaponry. A black gambler hat with digital dampener to prevent facial recognition sat atop white hair pulled into a tight ponytail. Hardened, customized armor covered her body and would stop a bullet as easily as it would diffuse an electronic bolt.

She caught sight of Moss and tipped her hat. "Hey, kid," she greeted. Though they had not seen one another for a week, she allowed no fanfare.

"Grandma," Moss said simply.

"Hear your meeting with Judy is set," she said, cutting to the chase.

Moss nodded. "Tomorrow. Ynna tell you?"

Sandra snorted a laugh. "She did. Between grousing about getting killed in your video game."

Moss laughed too. "Yeah, she was pissed about that. Did you remind her that it doesn't matter, and we got what we needed?"

"Sure did, not that it stopped her from cawing," Sandra told him. "Pretty sure she's working out her frustrations by knocking boots with your plump pal."

Moss smiled at that, happy for Gibbs. "He must be thrilled."

"Kid's like a dog with a bone," she stated.

Moss raised an eyebrow. "I see what you did there."

"Wish you didn't," she retorted, hiding a smile. "Need a drink."

"That we have," Moss said, pointing to a bar where volunteers were working in shifts to serve cocktails. "Could use a refill myself."

"How's your brain?" Sandra asked as they made their way to the bar.

Moss watched as his grandmother ignored the bartender, grabbed a bottle, pulled the spout out and took a swig. She nodded to the volunteer and they stepped away.

"My mind is still on the fritz," Moss admitted. "Getting worse, really. Pretty sure ThutoCo is trying to backdoor my brain. I've reached out to Jo about letting me see Patchwork to take a look at the programming in my chip."

"That'd be my guess too. Jo won't part with her boy easily after what he's been through. Most veterans want to keep their young from seeing the shit they have. I'll come along when you go see her," Sandra said as though she was offering, though Moss knew it was an order.

"Sounds good," he agreed.

Sandra looked at him with deadly seriousness. "And don't come back here tomorrow without Judy in tow. Tell 'em we need 'em and the time for wallowing is over. We've all lost loved ones, but we can't sit on this technology any longer."

"Meeting didn't go well?" Moss asked. Sandra had brought Anders, an off-worlder and pilot, to try and rally the distant planetary colonies to their cause. If she was still desperate to unlock Carcer's proprietary interplanetary communicator, which they had stolen, Moss knew the plea for help had not gone well.

Sandra gritted her teeth and growled, "No. The few remaining free colonies want proof of what we got before they'll strike a deal. Keep telling me it's as hard out in the stars as it is here on Earth… as though they have any fucking clue."

"I'll make sure Judy comes," Moss assured her.

She took another swig and handed him the bottle. "You do that."

CHAPTER 2

Moss knew that Ynna was still hungover the next afternoon.

She wore large sunglasses to cover the bags under her cybernetic eyes, set her microdyed hair to black and wore a ripped tee shirt, leather pants and combat boots.

"You know how I can tell you're hungover?" Moss asked with a wry smile.

"Because I'm too weak to put your face through the fucking wall for bringing it up?" she threatened in a half-joke that made Moss regret saying anything.

"No, because you're dressed like a normal person," he told her. Ynna had a style all her own and hardly ever appeared in public without wearing something she had tailored herself.

"Moss," she said, turning to face him as they approached the van. "I don't think I can accurately express how little interest I have in discussing my fucking wardrobe with you."

"Whatever there, Drinky," Moss joked as he opened the driver's side door for her. "Want me to drive?" He offered since she was clutching her coffee cup in two white-knuckled fists.

"Not on your life," she groaned, snatching the keys with her augmented hand. "Your jerkyass will make me rolf in a hot second."

"Couldn't you have just taken something for the hangover?" Moss asked as he climbed in next to her.

Turning on the car and starting to drive, she groused, "Don't you think that if I could have taken a pill and felt better I would have? We're all out of AfterJack so I'm stuck with this coffee."

She turned the key and started to drive. Hitting a pothole, the coffee spat out of the slit in the lid and onto her hand, and she hissed.

"So," Moss began but she shushed him.

"How about we have some quiet time for the drive?"

He waited just a moment.

"So," he began again with a childish grin. "How are you and Gibbs?"

She took a deep breath to calm herself before saying, "There is no *me and Gibbs*."

"Think he'd say the same thing if I asked him?" Moss asked, having a lot of fun annoying Ynna in her current state.

"Fuck, Moss," she whined.

He chuckled. "Sorry, sorry, I'll stop."

She pulled out a cigarette and lit it, dragging deeply. Wind gusting through the open window blew ash off the tip and showered Moss as they drove. They stayed silent until they reached their destination and parked. Ynna turned to Moss seriously.

"Listen to me, this is a hard place full of hard people. You need to be careful."

"I can take care of myself," Moss said.

"No, seriously," Ynna said. Her tone gave him pause.

"What is this place exactly?" he asked, his nerves beginning to get the better of him.

She took off her glasses and looked into him.

"Most people cannot afford Carcer protection. That company comes at a premium which your average citizen just can't pay. Your husband steals your kid, your apartment is looted, you get attacked, your account gets hacked, you need someone to help you. There are freelance private investigators, hatchetmen, breakers and lyers who can solve your problems. They get licenses from the mayor's office, a loophole Carcer has tried to close for years but which the voters will *never* approve."

Moss had heard all this before but did not want to interrupt Ynna.

"This place we are walking into is full of all those people. They don't like new faces or people trying to change the world. Their livelihood depends on nothing ever changing, so keep your head down and your mouth shut. We just need to convince Judy to come with us and get out."

She stamped out her cigarette in a stack of butts threatening to overflow a yellowed coffee cup. She was starting to seem like herself and Moss was grateful she was there.

"Just keep your head on a swivel."

"You too," he said, trying to sound confident and failing.

She smirked and pulled one loose strand of hair into the tie. "I always do."

They stepped from the car and Moss noticed dark gray clouds moving in under the almost-white clouds that were pulled as a sheet over the city. Reflecting off the glass-coated concrete buildings, the city was a grim monochrome.

More rains were coming. Ceaseless, relentless rains that made the world feel as if it were in perpetual night. He told himself it wasn't an omen of things to come.

He turned to the building: a cement square fronted with heavy rusted doors. The squat structure was dwarfed by the looming buildings all around it. The name, written in neon lights above the doors, read "The Pillbox" with the P flickering and going dark. Moss swallowed hard and Ynna cracked her knuckles against a metal palm.

"Ready?" she asked.

He looked at her, forehead creased in worry. "Less and less by the moment," he admitted. "Let's get this over with."

"Before you chicken out?" She joked with a little smile, looking as though her headache was mounting an offensive.

"Basically," he said sheepishly.

They approached the door and Ynna flipped her middle finger to the camera mounted above. The heavy metal moved more quickly than Moss had anticipated, and they strode forward into a square anteroom with another door and some unused pegs on the wall for hats and coats. Ynna slid a metal bar horizontally and pushed open the second door to reveal a room containing a confusing mix of antiquated and modern furnishings and fixtures.

Designed to look like a nineteen-forties bar, The Pillbox was full of wooden tables set with small lamps in the centers. Booths of ripped and patched vinyl lined the walls. Exposed wood pillars stretched from the checkered floor up to a ceiling of rust covered pipes. A long bar stretched along the rear wall, backed with dust-covered bottles. A sign hanging behind the bar read, "RULE 1: Be Courteous. RULE 2: Clean Up Any Blood You Spill." Moss hoped it was intended as humor but suspected it wasn't.

Ynna nudged him and gestured to a table. Judy sat there with a man he recognized but couldn't place. He was so happy to see Judy. They wore a large gray bomber jacket, mirror shades and had a new haircut: shaved bald along the sides with jet black dyed hair slicked down the center.

Moss and Ynna made their way through the heavily armed and armored patrons to the table.

"Philip," Ynna greeted the tired looking, gaunt man who sat with their friend. That jogged Moss's memory. He was Philip Tanner, a private investigator they had met when they were investigating Ryp the Jackr.

"Moss, Ynna," the older man said as he stood lethargically and began to leave. "Nice to see you both."

"You too," Ynna said, and Moss nodded to him as he moved away.

"I'd hug you," Ynna began saying to Judy.

They looked up, eyes covered by the glasses. "But you know better?"

"Judy," Moss blurted, unable to help himself. "I'm so sorry!"

Judy turned to him, their face hard. "I'm sure you are."

"I never meant for it to happen. I know my pain can never come close to yours, but I feel it too and I'm just so sorry."

"I'm happy you're sorry," Judy snorted. "But it won't bring him back."

Moss felt as though he had been stabbed in the chest. He had known this meeting wouldn't be easy, but he had hoped it wouldn't be like this either.

"I'm sorry too, Jude," Ynna said, sitting down across the table from them.

Judy shook their head. "Look, you found me, and you need something, so let's talk business."

"It doesn't have to be like this," Ynna said, deep sorrow and disappointment coating her words.

Judy scoffed. "The fact that you only came looking for me when you needed something tells me *exactly* how it is."

"We knew you wanted to be left alone." Ynna pointed an accusatory finger. "Plus, we had to save this dumb fuck."

"It's true," Moss said, trying to sound consoling even though the words stung. "We don't have to fight. We missed you and wanted you back. But Ynna is right, we were also trying to respect your wishes."

"My wish," Judy said, pulling the glasses from their face, "was for Stan to live."

"Me too," Moss said, their loss heightening his own.

His words were drowned out by Ynna nearly shouting, "Well, he didn't. He died. A lot of people died. My mom was shot and died in front of me. Then the man who was more like a father to me than my own died too. My brother died. I watched Bernard and Chicken Thumbs die.

"People fucking die. It sucks and it's brutal, but if we let it kill our spirits the assholes win! You're not dead and the other people who love you need you now more than ever."

Judy's face registered shock before softening ever so slightly. Moss would never have used the approach Ynna just had, but it seemed to work.

"You love me?" they asked softly. Judy had always been tough and hard as nails, but Stan had often told Moss that they had a soft side under it all. Until now, Moss had never truly seen it.

"Of course we do, idiot," Ynna told Judy and laid a hand on theirs.

Judy turned wet eyes on Moss. "We do," he agreed. "All we have is each other."

Judy smiled. It struck Moss how odd it was to be having this heartfelt moment in a place like this. Surrounded on all sides by drunk murderers.

"Thank you," Judy said softly. "And Ynna."

"Yeah?" She answered with a sweet smile to match.

Judy winked. "Sorry I killed you."

Ynna huffed and rolled her eyes. "Go fuck yourself."

"There it is," they laughed and chided, "Loved that 'female armor' you had on."

Ynna huffed. "I like looking good. Deal with it."

Moss piped up before Ynna got any more annoyed. "So, why Rome?"

Judy smirked, their eyes glistening happily at the memory. "I wanted to be a gladiator and didn't want to fight in the Bunny Holes."

Moss had heard of the incongruously named fighting pits in the Crow Town District of the city.

"I see," Moss said.

"The game offended your delicate sensibilities?" Judy mocked.

Moss shrugged. "A little," he admitted. "I mean, you know what happened to Verix? I captured her in-game, but some player somewhere had to experience in VR their own torture and rape before the triumph. It's fucking gross."

"People know what they are signing up for when they enter the game. Shit, they even pay that subscription fee for the pleasure. They want to experience a digital escape as grim as real human history. It's their prerogative. I'm sure the guy who was playing Verix was a masochist who loved what they got."

"I guess," Moss said, feeling a pang of guilt.

"It's what people want," they said. "They want to hurt others without actually hurting anyone in the real world. It may be hard to hear for a bub like you, but it's the truth of it. I mean, it's why I did it."

Moss let the silence hang, considering Judy's words. They were right, he knew, but it was ugly.

"Not for nothing," Judy added. "It was cool what you guys did in the game. A lot of people appreciated it."

"It's what we do," Moss said.

Judy smiled. "More and more, I am coming to understand the truth of that. But anyway, what's up?" Judy asked. "I know you didn't come here to discuss the finer points of digital morality."

Ynna still seemed to be sulking so Moss explained. "We got our hands on some tech we can't break. We will need both you and Patchwork to get it working."

"You really *are* trying to get the band back together," Judy observed.

Moss smiled. "We need everyone."

"Look," Ynna interjected. "I had two health potions left. If I had been playing with a neural link instead of the fucking keyboard Sandra could scrounge up, you wouldn't have been able to kill me."

Judy pounded the table and laughed. "Shit, you're a sore loser."

"It's a poor craftsman who blames their tools," Moss added with a chuckle.

"Oh, fuck off, bub," Ynna said, genuinely annoyed now.

Moss cocked his head. "Well, *I* wasn't killed," he said and, without thinking, held his hand up for a high five from Judy.

When they met his palm with theirs, he knew Stan would have been thrilled.

"Shit," Judy muttered as their eyes shifted to a man looking between them and his palmscreen.

"What?" Moss asked, seeing the man nudge his friend and nod in their direction.

"I fucked up," Judy said, hand moving to their weapon. "I asked two of the most wanted people on the planet to meet me at a bounty hunter bar."

More heads began turning as word spread.

"Oh, we're all kinds of fucked now," Ynna said, all hints of the hangover evaporating.

CHAPTER 3

Bounty hunters began to move toward their table. In a flash, Ynna was up and had the throat of one in her cybernetic fist. The tall hunter covered in glowing tattoos raised his hands defensively as her fingers closed around his neck. Moss pointed his kingfisher and Judy their rifle, but they were severely outgunned and surrounded.

"It doesn't have to be like this!" Judy announced to the room.

The massive bartender in his brown fur coat yelled, "Take this shit outside!"

"Let him go and we can talk," one of the other hunters said to Ynna. The man whose neck she held wheezed as his face turned deep crimson and his eye bulged.

Moss felt his heart thumping and grasped desperately for something to do.

The corners of his vision began to blur. "Shit, no!" he exclaimed before he saw white.

"Fuck!" he screamed in his hex. He was back in the program in his mind. The program that his family had designed and uploaded to the chip in his brain had been on the fritz since he had used it to escape from the Carcer facility in Africa.

"Kiddo?" Moss heard from over his shoulder. He turned to see the digital construct of his father that his father himself had put into the program. He hadn't appeared for a long time and Moss was thrilled to see him. Seeing his father as a vision of his former self made Moss forget everything happening in the outside world.

"Dad!" he cried as he embraced his father.

Tears streamed down both their faces and they stood in silence for a while until his father pulled away.

"How's it going?" he asked, so casually it made Moss laugh.

Then he remembered where his body was. "Well, dad, not great. I think I'm about to get into a gun battle with a bar full of bounty hunters."

His father's expression changed to one of terror as the color drained from his face. Moss again marveled at how real a recreation of himself his father had crafted.

"Oh, goodness, Mossy, what are you doing here then?"

Moss's head fell. "I can't control it," he admitted. "I'll explain, we have time."

"We do?" his dad asked, the concern still evident in his voice and fear in his eyes.

Moss nodded. "This program has been glitching out on me, so we ran some tests. When I'm in here, time outside doesn't really pass. It's like a thought and takes less time than a blink. If, however, I use the program to engage with the outside world, time passes normally within as without."

His father furrowed his brows but nodded in understanding. "I see. You weren't kidding when you said this program was so much… so much *more* than I realized."

Moss laughed. "You have no idea. Shit, *I* have no idea. Mom took your program and injected it with steroids."

Moss's father rubbed his face with his hands. "Your mother," he remarked and trailed off a moment. "I love her but doing this to you is dangerous. We were supposed to be the people in your life who protect you!"

His cheeks flushed crimson, but Moss put a reassuring hand on his shoulder. "Honestly, it has."

"Says the kid about to be shot by a room full of bounty hunters," his dad noted with a sorrowful smile, beginning to pace around the room.

Moss let a smile cross his own lips. "Oh, well, I *am* the most wanted man on the planet," he half-joked.

"Oh, Moss," his father said, collapsing onto a couch. "What did we do to you?"

Moss sat beside his father. "You showed me the world for what it is, and now I'm doing the same for others. Sure, I'm scared all the time, I've been shot, I'm being hunted by the world's largest companies and I've committed mass murder in self-defense, but I'm doing something important. This world is all but enslaved and I'm working to free it.

"This program was a gift. Not just to me but to everyone. You've opened my eyes and soon, the planet's. It's a remarkable thing," he said, and he meant it. His faith in what they were doing oscillated frequently but right now, he knew how important the work they were doing was.

His father let out a long sigh. "I'm happy about all that, truly, but. . . " he paused, looking for the words. "As a parent, you spend your whole life worrying about your child. You just want to keep them safe, no matter the price. Fighting ThutoCo cost your mother and me, the real me, the chance to watch you grow up and become the man you are.

"So, while I couldn't be prouder of what you are doing, it also pains me to know the peril I put you in. Does that make sense?"

"It does," Moss told him quietly. He sighed and wrung his hands. "I guess that's just something I can't really relate to yet."

"Maybe not," his father agreed. "Any news on that front?"

Moss grimaced, hating that he kept being asked about his love life. "No, Dad."

"Alright, I won't press you," he said with a little smile. "Just don't wait too long. When all is said and done, family is one of the most important aspects of life. I created a personality mapping system which was thought impossible for generations, but in the end, the best thing I ever made was you."

Moss began to weep. He was so happy to have this version of his father back and so sad to have lost the real man. He wanted more than anything to have his father back and to speak with him. Though Moss knew how lucky he was even to have this, it wasn't the same as having the real thing.

"Dad," he croaked. "Where have you been?"

His father wiped tears from his cheek and looked at Moss miserably. "I don't know. It sounds like this program has changed a lot since I first created it. I don't understand how I work well enough to explain it and when you aren't here, I don't exist, I just," and he made a clicking sound, "disappear."

"Yeah," Moss said, thinking about the nature of the program.

"It's just like being dead," his father observed. The silence hung heavy for a moment before he looked at his son and asked, "So, why do you think you are here?"

Moss had been asking himself the same thing. "I enter the program when I get overwhelmed," he explained. "It just happens. I don't know why you are here this time, though."

"Other than the firefight you think is about to happen?"

Moss smirked. "Right, other than that."

"You know I was never a proponent of violence?"

"I know," Moss sighed, somehow feeling like he was being lectured.

His father tapped his temple. "Brain always defeats brawn."

Moss shrugged. "That has not always been my experience."

"Well," his father began but the world turned black.

Moss heard the confused noises in the room and knew he was back in the real world.

The screens that filled the bar fired up and the room was bathed in an unnatural glow. A face Moss recognized materialized on all the screens and a shiver ran through him.

All the faces in the building turned to look at Warden Ninety-Nine, the man who had shot Ynna and captured Moss in Carcer City. He grinned devilishly on the hacked screens.

"Greetings, freelancers," he said, the friendly greeting belying his vile intent. "We have a force gathered outside this establishment. You have within three wanted criminals. If you turn them over to us, we will forgo our policy against paying non-Carcer staff and pay their bounties in full. This is a one-time offer and should you choose to refuse, we will take the criminals by force."

More guns were raised as Moss watched the thought of massive payouts fill the eyes of the hunters. Money symbols literally flashed on the digital faceplate of one.

"You have three minutes," the warden concluded, and the clamor of voices filled the room as all the hunters moved in. Everyone was shouting and pointing weapons until Moss raised his hands, letting the weapon spin on his fingers.

"All right!" he shouted and the room fell silent. Ynna and Judy looked at him in shock. "You can take me in."

"What the fuck?" Ynna muttered under her breath as all the hunters moved in.

"But who is going to do it?" Moss asked, his father's words still fresh in his mind.

The corner of Judy's mouth turned up, understanding washing over their face. "Carcer won't let you all split the bounty," they observed. "They probably won't even give one of you the bounty, but definitely not a hoard."

The hunters all began to eye one another suspiciously.

"I'll take him," one man said. Tall and strong with a cleft pallet and two cybernetic arms, he strode forward as he made his pronouncement.

A wiry woman pointed a pistol at him. "Like hell you will, Joysticks! I'll take him."

At that, the room erupted once more until Moss fired a shot into the ceiling, his blue bolt sizzling against the concrete and sending a cloud of dust showering down. The room quieted again.

"Or," Moss shouted, knowing that he would not be able to silence the trigger-happy group another time, "You can help us escape."

"Now, why would we do that?" Joysticks intoned ominously.

Moss smiled. "Money," he said. "We will pay every single one of you my full bounty if you get us out of here."

Another voice came from somewhere in the crowd. "Some good the money will do us if Carcer puts a bounty on our asses."

This elicited many nods. Moss's heart pounded and his hands shook. If he couldn't sell this, all would be lost. He would be killed or taken and there was no way he would be lucky enough to escape another time.

"Carcer couldn't afford to put bounties on all of you," Moss explained, trying to sound cool but the words trembled. "In this room are the finest lyers in the city. If Carcer put you all out of work, the citizenry would revolt. Carcer needs you lot to take all the small jobs they can't. They may pretend to hate you, but they need you. You know this as well as I do. Help us and you'll be richer and," he added for good measure, "who among you wouldn't like to stick it to Carcer?"

Smiles began to cross the faces of many in the room until the same voice from the back yelled, "You have the money?"

Ynna let the man in her grasp go. "Oh, we will get you the money and you can expect more if you help us in the future too. Carcer *might* pay one of you once, but we will pay all of you forever."

Joysticks held a gun to Moss's temple as the door opened and a warden strode in. Moss was disappointed but not surprised to see that it was not Ninety-Nine. The warden was clad all in black with the visor down on her helmet.

"Hand the criminal over and we will remit payment," she commanded, taking no note of all the hunters around the room.

"No," Joysticks boomed as the bartender pressed the button to close the front door. "You pay and I'll hand him over. I know how you corporate hacks work."

The warden took another step forward. "You don't set the terms here," she said with cold calculation. "You will hand him over and we will pay you outside," she began as Ynna slipped behind her wearing only a bra and panties.

When coming up with the plan, Judy had scoffed that Ynna "never missed an opportunity to get undressed."

As the warden continued to speak, Ynna came up behind her and slit the warden's throat through the soft part of the armor at the neck. She held the helmet under the crook of her elbow as the body slid to the floor so the mounted camera would not register the death.

"I don't trust you. I don't believe you will pay me," Joysticks said, continuing to vamp so the Carcer operatives watching the remote feed wouldn't get wise. Ynna slid into the helmet and several hunters began moving the Carcer armor from the Warden's body onto Ynna. She struggled to stay still as Judy helped pull on the vest and clip on the plates.

The hunter who had offered to take the place of a male warden began doing calisthenics in his orange thong rather than getting dressed and Moss was relieved that the warden had been female.

Ynna gave a thumbs up at her side and Joysticks said, "All right, I'll hand him over, but I expect to be paid now."

He shoved Moss toward Ynna who grabbed him and spun him toward the door.

Joysticks followed closely behind as Ynna forced Moss outside by the neck.

Fear gripped him as he saw just how surrounded they were. The street had been blocked off on both sides; four Carcer vehicles hovered overhead with spotlights pointed down, and a van sat at the center of the action. Countless officers had their weapons raised. A few faces peeked from the surrounding buildings, nervously watching the scene unfold. Garbage blew down the street and clothes hanging on lines twirled as a cold breeze washed up the street.

Moss felt that they had made a terrible mistake.

CHAPTER 4

"I have the terrorist Moss," Ynna announced.

There was no fanfare, no cheering from the assembled officers, just raised weapons.

The rain that had started to fall while they were inside whipped around them, flung in every direction by the thrusters on the cars. It splashed against Moss's face, forcing him to squint, and plunked loudly off every surface.

It was a tense stand-off and Moss was as nervous as he had ever been. He had seen a lot of action, more death and firefights than he cared to count; but looking at all the weapons pointed directly at them, he didn't know if he would survive this one.

Ynna tapped his neck and he braced for what would come next. He heard the click of the grenade, heard Ynna count in her mind and felt her push him. Falling to the ground, he covered his ears as she kicked the grenade toward the van.

She had timed it perfectly and the grenade counted down just as it struck the side of the vehicle. Rain and bodies were blasted in every direction as the van exploded. The street rocked as steaming shrapnel screamed through the rain. The unhurt Carcer officers ducked and the hovering patrol vehicles banked, spraying smoke, steam, water and blood in every direction. Moss's ears rang and his heart pounded.

The hunters inside The Pillbox began to pour out in a cacophony of cheers, curses and gunshots. These people lived for chaos and violence and immediately joined in the madness. One hunter detonated a grappling rocket, massive teeth firing from both sides of a shoulder-mounted cylindrical tube. The rear of the tethered teeth chewed deep into the cement and the other side grabbed one of the cars. A cable began to winch within the tube, sending the vehicle careening through the sky like a fly pulling against a web. The onboard computers tried to correct but the car swung wildly before striking the one to its left.

Both came crashing to the ground, shaking the earth as Moss got to his feet. The hunters and officers were exchanging fire at an alarming rate, shells pouring to the ground and hissing as they bounced against the slick sidewalk.

The man in the thong made a run for a group of officers shooting from behind a little wall they had erected. His tattoos seemed to dance as he sprang over the wall and pounced on the officers, his two nanoblades sinking into them with ease. Like a wild predator, he pulled the blades free, showering himself in blood. He whooped, eyes wild, and made his way toward the other officers.

Ynna handed Moss a gun and Judy was on them in a moment, chunks of bullet-ridden wall coming down around them. More hunters rushed out of the bar, and one woman used her cybernetic legs to leap onto the one remaining flighted car, punching through the windshield with a robotic arm to drag out the driver and toss him screaming to the ground. If his body made a sound when it crunched against the sidewalk, it was inaudible over the gunfire.

Moss wondered if the fourth car had fled, if the driver had taken manual control and "gone for help," though they would have undoubtedly already called for backup.

A hunter firing shots down the street was shredded by a machine gun, blood spraying everyone around him.

Moss took a few useless shots as Judy all but dragged him away from the scene.

This whole thing was a distraction for escape and now they needed to get away. Joysticks turned back to them as they moved to flee, calling, "We had better get fucking paid."

Four more officers rounded a corner as the three ran down the street. Ynna shot two before they even registered what was happening. Judy tossed a dart which whistled through the air, striking one and detonating instantly, and leaving two bodiless sets of legs on the rain-slicked street.

"I've got a ride around back," Judy said before adding, "we aren't out of this yet."

As Judy guided them to a sleek black car in the style of old muscle cars, Ynna snorted, "I can't believe you used to be one of those Carcer assholes, Jude."

Judy shook their head as they opened the driver's side door. "You really want to compare histories, Silver Spoon?"

Moss shook his head as he moved to open the door and get in. They hadn't been followed but he didn't know how long they had before Carcer sent more men. The hunters were likely getting out of there as well, so time was short.

He felt a shooting pain in his side as he climbed into the vehicle. He put his hand on the pain and was surprised to find blood coating his palm. "Shit," he said. "I've been shot." He hadn't felt anything in the clash, but now that he was aware of it, the pain radiated from the spot.

"Ugh," Ynna scoffed. "When *haven't* you been shot?"

"Shit," Moss murmured again as Ynna slid over and began tearing his shirt open.

He saw the program flash in his vision.

"Don't go there," Ynna warned. The car was already lifting, lurching into the sky with a false revving of a diesel engine from some internal speaker. "We gotta get him to a doctor."

"Already on it, but we've got company," Judy called back as the car started to haul ass.

Now it was Ynna's turn to holler "Shit" as flashing lights rapidly gained on them.

"Old girl's got a few tricks up her sleeve," Judy said.

Moss focused on the car, on the swinging lights and on Ynna. He didn't want to dip back into the program, didn't want to disappear from the world into his mind.

The car shook as a rocket fired from somewhere within the car. He saw a blinding light and heard the nearby crash.

"Keep pressure on it," Ynna demanded. She pulled a long, digital scoped rifle from hooks in the backseat. Moss knew he was fading but couldn't help but appreciate how prepared Judy was for this eventuality.

He tried to hold on to his mind, to cling to reality as Ynna fired shots out the window. Air ripped through the cab as Judy turned the vehicle hard to avoid fire. The car crunched against a building and ripples of pain shot through Moss's body as it contorted on impact.. Glass and rain poured down on the car as the world flew by.

The speed and movement were making him sick.

Ynna pulled sopping hair out of her face as she tried to target their pursuers to no avail. Wind and rain constantly slapped her hair into her face.

Moss tried to speak but no words came.

His hex was moving in around him. At least he would be with his father if he … and he wondered then if he was about to die?

As so often in the past, his mind faded into the program.

In his hex, he felt no pain.

His father wasn't there.

He was alone. Standing from his bed, he moved to his console. He knew that the program would use his neural link to connect with the outside world. He thought about calling Gibbs. Considered calling his grandmother. But in the moment, he only wanted to talk with one person.

Izzy didn't answer.

He began to sob, digital tears rolling down his face.

He felt a hand on his shoulder.

"Hey, Dad," he said, turning to look.

His mouth fell open. This was impossible.

Standing before him was not his father, but his mother. She looked exactly as he remembered her, exactly as she did in the pictures he had of her. Young and beautiful and full of life. A short black bob framed a freckled face. Her girlish features belied her strength and intelligence.

She smiled and his heart melted. Everything but her radiant face, full of a mother's love, dropped away. If he died now, he would die happy.

"Hey bubba bear," she said, and he wrapped her up in a hug he never wanted to leave. He had to lean down for the embrace, having been taller than her from the time he was eleven.

After what may as well have been an age, he asked the only thing he could think to ask,: "How?"

"Couldn't tell you," she said.

"You aren't in the program," Moss told her. He knew that much. For as many surprises as this program held, he knew she wasn't in it.

"I guess I am," she said, but the revelation was not helpful.

"No," Moss said. "You aren't. I know you aren't. You wouldn't let yourself be."

She shrugged, and though he was still as happy to see her as he could have been to see anyone, a fear started creeping into his mind.

"What do you remember?" he asked. "Tell me about your last days or something."

She shook her head, her flat black hair hardly moving and her dark eyes piercing his. "I don't remember that. I remember when you came home from school that day, when the teacher had pulled you aside to tell you that your drawing was the best in the class. You were so happy. I was so proud."

Moss felt a searing pain and his head striking metal. He reached out mentally and physically for his mother, but she was gone. The moment was gone. He didn't know if he would ever see her again. He cried out in pain and sorrow.

"Get him up." Judy's voice.

His body was lifted, rain pounding his face. Blurred buildings and faces filled his vision.

It had only felt like a moment in the program, but time had passed. That was unusual.

The rain relented as they entered some structure.

Then he saw nothing. No program, no dreams, nothing.

"Welcome back, Moss," a computerized voice said in a soothing tone.

"What?" All he saw was white light. He felt no pain, but he could tell that he was not in the program.

The suspicion was confirmed when he heard, "I swear, if we have to patch you up one more time."

"Hey, grandma," he uttered, closing his eyes. "Where am I?"

"Sawbones," she informed him. "Wasn't as bad a hit as we thought. Good news too, cuz we have shit needs tending to."

He opened his eyes again and they began to focus. He saw large mechanical spider arms with a screen at the center. The computer-generated face of a doctor was in the middle. It reminded him of the 'doctors' he had back in the burbs. They had exclusively used computer doctors there and Moss had never even known humans had done the job until he was in the city. The realization was another reminder of how much his life had changed, how much he had changed.

"AI doc?" he asked.

"AI partner," said an unfamiliar woman's voice with a subtle Cantonese accent. He looked over to see a diminutive woman in scrubs. He blinked a moment, thinking she was his mother, but as she moved into focus he realized of course, she wasn't.

"I saw my mom," he said toward where Sandra's voice had emanated. "In the program."

"Couldn't have been," she said. "Must have been a dream."

"Okay," Moss said, worried about the answer — about the line between his mind and the program. But he could press the issue later. He was tired and drained and really wanted to go back to sleep.

"Think you can walk?" Sandra asked, a hint of impatience in her voice.

Moss groaned. "I was just shot."

"I know you got shot, I'm standing right here," she said. Her gruff style usually didn't bother Moss, but in that moment he wasn't in the mood for it. "Wasn't what I asked."

Moss moved. He was groggy but felt as though he could walk. "Fine," he said in resignation. He looked around the sterile room. The AI doctor loomed over a square of white walls with a viewing window. Computers lined one side, and another was set with a metal cabinet full of little cubbies from which the robotic arms could grab surgical supplies. A holoprojected rendering of himself floated above him, displaying the exact nature of the wound both inside and out.

In the harsh light, Moss's grandmother looked old. Her leathered skin was creased with age, her frown lines cast deep shadows on her face and her hair was thin and opaque. Looking at her, Moss realized something: he was truly exhausted. It wasn't the physical fatigue of having been shot, patched up, pumped full of drugs and made to stand, but a deep internal exhaustion.

The relentless pace of a life into which he had been thrust came crashing down on him as he stared into the eyes of the aging warrior before him. She always reminded them that they were soldiers, and this was the way of things when engaged in a pitched battle, but Moss felt he had nothing left.

No motivation.

No reason to keep fighting.

All the things he had told his father, the things he had convinced himself of, were gone in a flash.

He was still a young man, but he had seen and done so much.

He had expected to live and die in the burbs, contributing little to the world except a few ThutoCo Productivity Points. Now, infused with a program that plagued his mind but which could also help free the people of the planet, he was forced to act.

Sandra's face did not fall or grow sympathetic as his own began to contort with the waves of misery and weariness crashing down upon him. She was the fighter he would have to be, the thing he became when forced. But she was also something he feared he wasn't.

He could fight, kill, do what needed to be done when he had to, but it drained the Moss he had thought he was. He wondered if these fears were byproducts of the program. Was his father's terror over what he was becoming bleeding into his psyche? Or perhaps ThutoCo breakers had breached the program? Or maybe he was simply scared?

He felt the floor rush up to meet him. His hands crunched against the cold tile as he collapsed. The cybernetic legs had tried to brace his fall, but the weakness had come from his mind and overridden their programming.

"Ain't got time for all this," his grandmother said as she hooked an arm under his chest, lifting him to his feet.

He gasped for air as his mind drowned.

"Give him a second!" Gibbs's voice cried out. A tinny version piped through a speaker. His friend's words only served to deepen his sorrow. Gibbs had come along to help and had been dragged down as deep as Moss.

The room began to spin but Moss felt hands on his face.

Sandra penetrated him with blue eyes. Those eyes that had seen war, watched her own body age in a cage. That had been swollen shut with beatings as she had counted days with scratches on her prison wall.

"I'm right here," she told him. She seemed to see him now. See his pain and his fear. She had brought him back from the brink before.

His eyes fluttered as the robotic arms unfolded and propped him up.

He heard a commotion just before seeing Gibbs and Ynna burst into the room. Ynna's influence on Moss's friend was clear. The young man had tended to wear jeans and picture shirts but was now dressed very differently. He wore tapered cargo pants loose at the top and nearly sprayed on by the ankle. His shiny black top was uneven and wrapped, held together with countless straps, some functional, some for show. The long sleeves telescoped down his arms and his orange hair was pulled into spikes. Moss smiled weakly; his pal looked good.

"We are all here," Sandra assured him. The toughness dropped a moment, replaced by a grandmother. "Because of you and *for* you."

Moss watched as Gibbs laced his fingers into Ynna's for reassurance. It was what he needed in that moment more than anything. More than his grandmother's shift in tone or her words, he needed to see some good. One small thing that reminded him that there was some hope left, that the actions he took could have a positive impact. This trivial moment shared by an absurd couple heartened him just enough that he felt he could keep going. It would pass, he knew, but it was enough for now.

Turning to the human doctor who had been silently watching the scene unfold, he asked, "Did you see anything unusual in my neural implant?"

She cocked her head, referring to the tablet on a nearby shelf. "No," she said. "Standard ThutoCo technology."

Moss nodded. "Okay."

"If you have concerns, there are medical professionals who specialize in neural interfacing," she suggested.

Moss nodded again. He had no interest in some technician from the corporate medical establishment tinkering in his mind. He assumed the woman standing in her lab coat was helping them off the books, but he couldn't risk further invasion. If someone was going into the program in his mind, it would have to be someone he trusted.

"You going to be okay?" Gibbs asked in a quavering voice.

"Not doing a great job hiding your concern," Moss chided gently, and smiled at his friend.

Ynna grinned. "I tell him that shit all the time! Man, I would love to play poker with you, I would take everything you own!"

Gibbs gave Ynna a sidelong glance. "We could play strip poker," he said, and winked.

The exchange, too, made Moss happy. Their banter annoyed some others in the crew and Sandra sighed in annoyance, but it filled Moss up.

He looked at Gibbs and thought of a television show he had made Moss watch and said, "What's next?"

Gibbs beamed.

PART II

CHAPTER 5

Moss and Sandra were on their way to the Talisman Saloon.

It would be a while before they arrived to re-enlist Patchwork. The breaker would be more valuable now than ever. When they first met, Moss had watched Patch easily hack one of the major companies and steal its funds. In addition to investigating the program, they needed the young man to pay all the bounty hunters.

"So," Moss began a little nervously. "What the hell?"

Sandra smiled at that. "Yes?" she asked, raising an eyebrow.

"You had to know what we were walking into.".

"I did," she admitted without a hint of shame or remorse.

"Then what the hell?" Even to his own ears he sounded like a petulant child, but he didn't care. He resented walking into a trap and being shot again.

"I knew you would make your way out of it," Sandra said plainly. "You are a smart young man, and you need to realize the leadership potential I see in you or this whole operation is for nothing."

"It was another test?" he howled. "Haven't I proven myself enough?"

"If you have to ask that question, you know the answer."

Moss thought back to a math class he had taken in the burb, shortly after his parents had disappeared. To the great consternation of the class, the teacher had announced that there would be a quiz at the end of every week. The students had groaned but the teacher explained, "If I quiz you every week, you will have to learn as we go and keep pace with my instruction. You will hate it, but come time for your final, you'll thank me."

What had shocked Moss at the time was that she was right. He had hated the quizzes, but by the end of the course he hardly had to study because he knew all the material.

"Fine," he snorted. "A little heads up would have been nice."

Sandra smirked. "If I had told you what you were gonna be walking into, you would have tried to come up with some cock and bull plan. As it was, you went in and had to think on your feet. You did and assuming we can get some money, you even secured us some new allies in the fight to come. You may hate my methods, but trust me when I tell ya they work."

Moss chuckled in exasperation. "Worked so good I got shot."

"Oh, quit yer bitching," Sandra snorted. "You're gonna get a lot worse than shot before all this is through."

"Aren't you just a ray of sunshine."

"Sun hasn't shone on this planet for a long time, kid. That's the point of all this. These companies blot out the light just like these buildings. People of this world gave over their lives in exchange for a couch and a remote. This is gonna be ugly, has been ugly, but change, true change, always is. You and that program in your brain are the dawn of a new day. You need to wise up and realize that before it's too late."

Moss didn't say anything; he just considered her words. He knew she liked to give speeches like this and he knew that he liked to hear them — to remind himself what this was all about. It was not just small moments of kindness, it was a movement.

"There is a promise on this planet and we fix to see it realized," Sandra concluded.

Moss nodded. He knew she was right. "Yes," he said. "But that doesn't mean it's always going to be easy for me."

"Nope," his grandmother agreed. "It's going to be hard and hardest of all for you. It's why I have to push you while I'm still above ground. My job is to make you tough enough to face whatever comes your way. I'm your family and I love you and that's precisely why I need to see you become the man you need to be. It'll be brutal and you may grow to hate me, but it'll be worth it."

"I'll never hate you," Moss said quietly. "I may hate your methods, but I'll never hate you."

"Here's hoping," Sandra said.

Moss stared out the window at the grimy streets below the elegant corporate towers. People in their tattered clothes stood in long lines for a coffee or made street deals for the pick-me-up to get them through the day. Vendors sold muffins made with bioprinted yeast and hotdogs with vat grown meat products as ads flashed all around them blaring 'stream the newest episode' and 'escape the drudgery with a new house in the MI.'

The city became more ramshackle as they flew. Nearing the Talisman Saloon, the tall buildings were replaced by massive stretches of once-squat homes now layered with corrugated tin apartments atop, reaching like rust-covered broken fingers into the gray sky. The copious weeds growing from the cracked streets clawed through layers of garbage. Lights flickered if they worked at all. People littered the streets, talking and jostling one another or gathering around screens pulled out into the road, sitting on broken-down furniture.

As the car landed, Moss noticed that an armed drudge had been placed on the landing pad to protect incoming vehicles.

"Things getting that bad?" Moss asked.

Sandra smiled. "That *good*. Folks are starting to see the companies for what they are and are fighting back. If the companies feel the need to defend themselves, you know we're having an impact."

Moss smiled and his grandma added, "You're having an impact."

Hardly anyone took note as they disembarked. Two more hard-looking street warriors were nothing new in Old Oak. Moss's clothes were stained and ripped from gunfire. The scent of his drying blood mixed with that of decaying garbage and sizzling meat from open cooktops on the counters in the storefronts. He felt safer in the places where the citizens ran the streets. It was a far cry from how he had felt when he first entered the city. He had been so frightened of the denizens who now brought him comfort.

The neon bull's head above the wooden doors to the bar hissed and popped with years of neglect, one of the horns having burned out entirely. They entered and heard the familiar sound of slow western music playing on an ancient jukebox. The patrons paid them as little mind as had the people on the street, most of them nursing drinks while staring absently at the screens installed around the walls above pictures of bison and cowboys mounted on faded wallpaper styled to look like wood paneling. The floor was sticky and felt like it could collapse under their weight at any moment.

A man was standing behind the bar wearing only tattoos and a somber expression. He didn't greet them. He simply pointed at the back of the bar and said, "She's upstairs. Hope you're here to help."

Moss felt himself tense. Something was wrong.

Sandra nodded and the two set off up the stairs to where Jo lived above the bar. It felt like a lifetime ago when Moss had last been here, begging Jo for help and having to tell her that Carcer had taken her son. Sandra didn't knock on the closed door, choosing to just walk right in. Jo was sitting at the end of a small bed with aged linens. The only window in the room had been boarded up and a small lamp sitting on a large spool being used as a bedside table provided only dim light.

Jo looked up at them with wet eyes, her face contorting in anger at seeing them.

"He with you?" she asked, her words both terrified and hopeful.

Sandra shook her head and Moss swallowed hard.

"Me and mine have seen nothing but trouble since you and Burn first shadowed my door," Jo snapped at Moss. He knew she was right.

"Listen, if you've got troubles," Sandra said with uncharacteristic kindness, "we'll sort it."

Jo stood, the spurs on her boots jingling. She wore black leather pants and a black vest over a white tank top. Her long dreadlocks dangled around her face. "Oh, I know you'll sort it because I also know you're sure as shit not here to see me."

Sandra held up her hands defensively. "You're right. We are here for the boy, but if he's in some trouble, you should be happy it's us who's here."

Jo gritted her teeth. "Don't you tell me how to feel when you've got your kin beside you and mine is missing."

Moss had never heard anyone speak to his grandmother that way. He knew the two women served together during the war, but thought Jo had only been a junior officer who would never have spoken to a superior like this. But the war was long over and things were very different now. He was also surprised by the deference Sandra showed the woman even if they needed something from her.

He couldn't help but remember his own digital father's concern about himself. He and Patchwork were young, and though he knew they were doing something important, he understood that their parents simply wanted them to be safe.

"I've lost a child," Sandra said. "Won't let it happen to you."

"I see you, Sandra, don't think for a second I don't," Jo snarled. "But I'll take your help since I haven't seen my son for days now."

"He been breaking?" Sandra asked, ignoring the accusatory tone.

Sandra rolled her eyes. "I have hardly a clue what that boy gets up to, but I know it ain't good."

Moss cleared his throat. "It *is* good. Patchwork does nothing but good."

Jo's face softened slightly. "You're just like him. Just as much the dope as he is. You boys think you're doing good but you're also playing the fool if you think you'll fix this world."

"*I* ain't some fool kid," Sandra snapped. "And we *will* fix this world!"

"No, Sandra, you'll die trying," Jo said, misery overwhelming her words so they sounded more sad and true than mean.

"Haven't died yet. Tell us what you know and we'll get Willis back."

Jo nodded slowly, running a fingernail over a scar on her forearm. "I don't know anything. He said he was going out the other night and didn't come back, hasn't come back."

"You know any of his friends?" Moss asked quietly.

Jo shook her head. "I've never known his friends. They are all online. I know that's part of the reason he jumped into Burn's arms. He wanted some real people in his life who weren't me or his sister. These kids live their whole lives behind screens and in text, but it's all an illusion. Ain't healthy. I couldn't be there for him the way a mother should. I worked to keep him fed but it wasn't enough. I should have made him go outside, kick a ball, run around.

"I didn't and now look what's happened." Jo was lost in a sea of regret. Moss wondered what his real parents would say if they could see him now.

"You did what you could, Jo," Sandra said soothingly, her tone unfamiliar and unnatural but kind nevertheless. "We all got fucked when we got out and you made a life for your family. You kept 'em fed and that's more than we can say for a lot of folks.

"From what I hear he's also smart and capable and that's a testament to you."

Jo remained distant.

"He can do things no one else can," Moss added. "He's… he's remarkable."

Jo smiled as a tear ran down her face. "Thank you."

"We'll find him," Sandra said in a way so honest that no one could doubt her. "Even if I didn't need him, I'd find him for you."

Jo looked right into Sandra's eyes. "You fixing to take him with you?"

Sandra nodded and Jo's head dropped in resignation. "Maybe you'll keep him safer than I can."

"Sometimes it's safer on the field than on the sideline," Sandra told her.

Jo snorted a miserable laugh. "You never did understand sports."

Sandra shook her head slowly. "Suppose I don't. Mind if we go in the kid's room?"

"That'd be fine."

Moss and his grandmother turned to leave the room. "And Sandra," Jo said in what amounted to a whisper. "Thank you."

"Don't thank me just yet," Sandra told her, the words hard.

"I'll thank you now *and* when I wrap my arms around my boy."

Patchwork's small room was exactly as Moss remembered. Old movie posters on the crumbling walls, a cot set in the corner with a blanket embossed with images of Japanese cartoons, a stinking spittoon filled to the brim with cigarette butts and an advanced computer on a folding table with an expensive black and yellow leather gaming chair sitting alongside.

"What you think?" Sandra asked.

"Nothing good," Moss said. "Patch loves to fuck with bigwigs so there's a long list of people who would like to see him … deactivated."

Sandra picked a pack of Longporks off Patchwork's desk and lit one with the flip top lighter sitting beside. "Or someone could have wanted to activate him for their own purposes."

"There's that, too," Moss agreed, turning to the holoprojected keyboard on Patchwork's desk. He knew he didn't possess the skills to hack his friend's password and breathed a sigh of relief when a desktop appeared above the folding table being used as a desk.

"Must not have thought he would be gone long if he didn't even log out," Moss observed.

"Getting fishier and fishier," Sandra noted. "Anything we can go on?"

Moss brought up a browser, but the auto-delete feature was activated so there was no history. Moss opened the chat. He clicked through flirtatious conversations with various online entities before finding one that piqued his interest.

"What you got?" Sandra asked as she saw him reading.

Moss ignored her a moment. "It's a chat," he said. "With someone named Zip Thud."

"Plan on telling me what it's about?" Sandra asked, either missing or ignoring the implication of the name.

"They're clearly friends and it's about going to pick something up, but it doesn't say what or where. The conversation is short and I'm guessing Patch deleted the previous parts," he explained, waving his grandmother's smoke away.

"Reach out to the friend," Sandra ordered.

Moss let his fingers hover as he tried to think of what to say.

"Just tell the kid we are a friend of his friend and are worried."

"These breakers are clandestine and not trusting by nature. We need a more measured approach," Moss said, but he was gently pushed out of the way as Sandra typed the message.

An ellipsis appeared almost instantly before their images were projected on the screen. Moss turned away instinctively but Sandra just looked at the screen. A message popped.

ZIP THUD: holy shit. I knew Patch was good but didn't know he ran with such illustrious rabble rousers.

Sandra leaned in to type but another message appeared.

ZIP THUD: Corner of Fell and Divis. I'll approach you.

The chat closed.

"Trap?" Moss asked.

"Nah," Sandra said. "Thinkin' he just wants to meet someone he deems famous."

"Sure," Moss said, still not quite able to wrap his head around his own reputation.

CHAPTER 6

Moss and his grandmother stood on a bustling street in the shadows of tall, glass-fronted buildings. The skyscrapers, which had been offices long ago, had been converted to apartments when refugees flooded the city. As the disease overtook the world, fewer and fewer companies relied on in-person offices and changed their cubicles over to housing. Anyone who got a job would be given a mattress under a desk and live in their workplace. Rather than being miserable about the tiny space, most were simply happy to have a roof over their head.

Drones skittered between the structures and people met in front of restaurants for drinks in the guise of meetings. Sandra had bought them overpriced sandwiches from a vendor who wouldn't stop telling them about the "wonderful locally roof-grown spices in our famous aioli." Though Sandra just groused that the flakes kept getting stuck in her false teeth.

As they finished eating, a boy with a slender frame made his way straight toward them. Black boots, ripped designer jeans and a hoodie pulled over his head.

"Follow me," he said through a voice-augmented device that gave him an unnatural, synthetic low timbre. He guided them quickly into an alleyway, easily skipping around the cardboard lean-tos and jumping over the junkies. When there were no more lights or mounted cameras, and the buzz of local drones was in the distance, he pulled back his hood to reveal the face of a kid no older than fourteen with cybernetic plates and 8-bit digital eyes where his real ones would be. They blinked and he shifted nervously.

"You're Zip Thud?" Moss asked incredulously.

The boy put his hands on his hips in annoyance. "Yes. Just ask your girlfriend."

Moss couldn't help but chuckle at that and the kid seemed bothered by the response.

"Where are your parents?" Sandra asked.

The boy's lips became a straight line. He had black hair and dark skin, and even through the synthesizer, he had an unmistakable Middle Eastern accent.

"Dead," he told her flatly. "Where are your parents?"

Sandra's lips curled up in amusement. "Dead."

The kid looked at Moss.

"Mine too," he said, his heart breaking for the little kid who felt he had to act so tough. He probably did. With his parents dead, there was likely no one in the world to look out for him.

It was true for so many young people. The puppet government had little interest in providing them aid, and unless he was already working for a company, none would hire him or offer any assistance. Moss had to give him credit that he seemed to be doing well for himself, given the circumstances. Those plates didn't come cheap and they seemed to have been installed professionally, so he was obviously doing something right. Most young people in his position fell in with a gang, begged or stole on the streets or just lost themselves to death in digital worlds.

"So, what's up with Patch?" The little lost soul asked.

"We were hoping you could tell us," Sandra said.

The digital eyes narrowed. "I mean, we're friends online and shit but I only met the cat once."

Moss's heart broke once more. Patchwork had been a fast friend but Moss had not reached out to him since being back. If this kid who seemed to care so little was his close friend or a person he confided in, Patchwork really was alone in the world.

"He mentioned to you that he was going to pick something up. Do you know what it was?" Moss asked.

"Nah," the kid said with a finality that Moss found unnerving. They needed more to go on.

"Think you can do a little quick breaking and find out what he was after or where he was going?"

The kid gave a crooked smile. "Don't do nothing free. Especially not for famous rebels."

"If you know who we are, maybe you know it's best just to help us," Sandra suggested.

Zip Thud folded his arms across his slight chest. "Thought you guys were here to help the little man."

Moss laughed. "He's got us there."

Sandra shook her head. "Fine, you help us find him and there'll be something in it for you."

"That's better," the kid announced. "Let me run some scans. I know I can find you something."

His digital eyes closed and the two shifted uncomfortably, looking up and down the street as they waited.

"Think you're going to try and bring this kid in after we get Patch?" Moss asked absently.

Sandra nodded as she watched one of the bodies wrapped in a sleeping bag shift. "I'll take anyone who can help as this gets bigger."

"Figured," Moss said. The kid obviously heard them as the corner of his lip turned up.

"He seems like a good one," Moss said for his benefit. Flattery was a powerful motivator.

"Okay," the youth said. "He's after something called Corp's Bane. Gotta be some new hacking thing I haven't heard of. Looks like he found it at a street dealer in the Baytop Market. Place called Gnubs' Emporium. That enough to go on?"

"You did great," Moss told him and the kid lit up. Moss suspected it had been a long time since he had been praised.

"Coolio," the kid said, regaining his calm demeanor. "Anything else you need from a world class breaker, hit me up."

"We'll be in touch," Sandra said, and he smiled again. She added, "You're part of the revolution now."

He looked like he was going to break into dance and a tear drop appeared on his eye plate. "Thanks!"

The sun had set by the time they reached the market. The sound of water lapping beneath their feet was drowned out by shoppers haggling and shop owners shouting about their deals. The entire marketplace was set up on a structure built over what used to be a bay. As the city's population increased, people demanded more space and some long-bankrupt company built this as a gift to the populace.

The familiar smell of sea air mixed with those of unwashed people, cooking foodstuffs, spices and generators belching smoke.

There were weight limits on the spots the merchants could rent so there were few permanent structures. Food trucks were parked near the entrance but as they moved deeper into the open mall, it was all wood, tarps, tents and tin.

"Eyes! I've got eyes!" a man shouted from behind a table of cheaply made cybernetics. "See what you've been missing! All purchases come with a money back guarantee!"

"Yeah, fucking right," Sandra snorted. "You believe people go in for this shit?"

Moss shook his head. "People want to compete with machines for jobs and are willing to do a lot."

"For now," Sandra said as she pushed Moss to avoid having him step through a wet piece of floorboard to the water below.

Moss tripped over a line of electric cables strapped together with duct tape and wrapped in faded caution tape as he gawked at a tank full of genetically-modified bioluminescent lionfish. Colors pulsated through the striped animals. Moss knew they were unnatural, but was mesmerized nevertheless.

"You and animals," Sandra said with a hint of judgment.

"I love them," he said quietly. "Always have."

His grandmother's face softened. "I know it, but why?"

"I think it was growing up in such a synthetic world. Everything was concrete and plastic, carpeted or digital. I never saw the natural world except through the camera of my drudge or recreated in games," he said thoughtfully. "Everything was false but something in me always chased the real."

He thought about the moment between Ynna and Gibbs, the truth in it. "Humans desire the real, but we've done away with it almost entirely. I know it's part of why I am working so hard in this fight. I want to give the planet back to nature. I want people to be able to walk through the woods. See a bear and hear birds trill. The work those folks are doing at The Conservation are a part of that future."

Sandra smiled, her face a shimmering blue in the light from the tank. "That place really had an impact on you."

"More than you know," Moss said wistfully.

He had only been there a short moment and hadn't thought much of it at the time, but it had left an indelible impression on him. Those people, cut off from the rest of the world but trying to preserve something all but extinct, gave him hope for the future. Amy, that little girl obsessed with a nature she had never been out to see, deserved her planet back.

"Come on," Sandra said. "Let's go and keep working toward that future you want."

They kept moving and entered a circular open area with benches and tables illuminated with solar tube lamps. At the center of the circle was a large six-sided holomap with stall names, descriptions and locations. A group of well-dressed people stood at one, holding bowls of vat meat on rice and discussing where they should shop next. Moss took them to be tourists. Tourists who would be parted from their cash chips before too long.

He stepped up to one of the maps and looked up the stall Zip had mentioned. The entire mall was laid out like a wagon wheel with concentric circles of shops and long bisecting rows leading out from where they stood. As Moss zoomed in on the stall, the screen flashed and read, "Your map will return after a brief message."

Moss sighed.

"Have you considered emigration?" a handsome, chiseled, gratuitously naked man asked from inside a fabulous apartment with bay windows looking out over a lush vista. "Are you tired of cramped living, pollution, disease, joblessness and poverty on earth? If you answered yes to any of those questions, it's time you considered one of NeoVerge Industries' off-world housing options. New worlds and new jobs await you . . ." It would have continued but Sandra slapped SKIP AD the moment it appeared.

"Trade that leash on earth for one in the stars," she scoffed.

Moss couldn't help but wonder what it was like on other planets. "It's just as bad there?" he asked, looking upward to the black sky made starless by light pollution.

Sandra snorted. "Didn't really know 'til recently, but Anders has been filling me in. Same shit, different planet. Turns out man is man no matter where we set up shop."

"As disappointing as it is unsurprising, I suppose," Moss said, sounding sadder than he had expected.

They continued to amble along until they saw a bright sign for Gnubs' Emporium. The shop was different from those around it. Rather than being constructed of found materials or held together with wrapped barbed wire, the stall was constructed of light metal. A red bulb bathed the interior in a low, almost ominous light, making it difficult to see the goods within. But the kiosk had a digital display of items for sale next to the thick, wrought iron bars that protected the owner. A round, pockmarked woman wearing heavy robes and a head wrap glared at them as they approached. Heavy bags sagged under her narrowed eyes and a toothless scowl contorted her thin lips.

"That look is a warm fucking welcome," Moss said, unable to help making a joke.

"Let me do the talking," Sandra said, and Moss was happy to oblige.

Sandra stepped forward and the woman looked straight at her wordlessly. "You Gnubs?"

The woman grimaced. "What gave it away, the sign or these?" She held up a hand with a thumb rounded off just past the joint.

Sandra gave a false smile. "I meant no offense."

"Sure you did," she asserted and turned to look at Moss. "Not all of our mommies and daddies could afford to design us beforehand." She shot him a condescending smirk. He had told his grandmother that he wouldn't speak but the comment made him angry.

"You don't know me," he fired back.

"Sure I do, bub," Gnubs said with a wink. He felt his fist ball. He was so far removed from the burbs that he was surprised and annoyed that she identified his origins so quickly.

"We are here for Corp's Bane," Sandra said, trying to get the conversation back on the rails.

Gnubs rolled her eyes lazily. "Can't help you."

"Can't or won't?" Sandra asked, her annoyance beginning to show.

"Those aren't mutually exclusive."

"We are trying to find the man who bought it from you. He's a friend of ours and could be in trouble," Sandra explained quietly, but Moss could tell she wanted to punch through the glass.

Gnubs laughed, a mean, meaningful laugh. "Listen here. I'm not a search engine. I'm not giving out information on things I don't have, and I definitely wouldn't give out information on customers.

"If this person is such a good friend, why do you have to ask me about them? You look to me like the type apt to steal. If you aren't here to buy something, why don't you fuck right off?"

Moss watched his grandmother's body tense with anger. "Okay, you won't give information but . . ."

Gnubs cut her off.

"Nope, don't sell it either. I'm a businesswoman and my business is private," she said with a dismissive wave of her hand.

"Bitch," Sandra snarled as she turned to walk away.

"Cunt," Gnubs called after them.

Once they were out of earshot, Sandra turned to Moss. "I want to put her through a fucking wall."

"I'm right there with you," Moss agreed.

"But we gotta be smart," she said, trying to take a calming breath although it came out in ragged bursts. *Seti*, she communicated through the neural link to their eye in the sky. *You got any breakers on hand could do a quick job*?

They shifted uneasily a moment as a man walked by trying to sell them copper cables wrapped around his arms and legs.

Sorry, Sandy, everyone in the city is on one job or another, Seti informed them. *You like the nickname? I'm trying something new.*

I don't, Sandra said, her tone clear in Moss's mind's ear. *Everyone is working? No one can break away for just a moment?*

It's a bad time, Seti said. *You know Carcer has been cracking down and you aren't the only team out there. Could probably get you someone first thing in the morning.*

Sandra and Moss both groaned. *Forget it*, Sandra said and ended the communication.

"Let's get a drink," she added, and began walking down the tight path.

The sound of loud voices and raucous laughter filled the air as they approached The Tiki Tomb, an open-air bar lit with tiki torches. The wide bar was wood paneled with the name burned into a long piece of boat hull. The tables were similarly constructed out of old pieces of ship. The wait staff wore faux plastic grass skirts and only leis as tops. Some appeared to be of Hawaiian descent, but all were well-toned and attractive, banking on tips from drunk patrons who appreciated their state of undress.

Moss and Sandra sat, shifting uncomfortably on the hard seats.

"Gonna get fucking tetanus from this bench," Sandra grumbled as a digital display of the drink options appeared above a little metal projector at the center of the square table.

Moss studied the themed drinks until a pretty waitress approached. Even sitting across from his grandmother, Moss couldn't help but steal a glance at her exposed breasts as she stood beside the table. She wasn't even trying to cover up; the flower necklace that dangled from her neck simply hung in her cleavage.

Sandra took no note of his flushing face as she ordered two pineapple vodka humuhumunukunukuapuaas. More skin was exposed as the waitress turned with a flourish to retrieve the drinks, sending the skirt's grasses dancing apart. He felt his heart race just for a moment.

"What are we going to do?" Moss asked quietly as he turned back to Sandra.

She sighed. "Think you know."

Moss shook his head. "No."

"You know we need to," she stated bluntly.

"I can't," he told her.

"You can," she said. "You've doubted yourself before and I've always been right."

"No," he said again. "The program is getting too unstable. Too weird. I just can't."

"You gotta use the program to fix it," she said, trying to smooth him. "We need the kid to get the money and mend your head. This is the only way."

"I'm . . ." he began.

"I know you're scared. I'm scared too, and I hate that it's come to this, but our choices are scant here," she said.

He knew she meant it, but every time he dipped into the program he felt his control over it slipping away. He still didn't know how he had seen his mother in there and what that could possibly have meant. The line between his own mind and the constructs of the program were becoming so muddy that he hardly knew what was his anymore.

His hand trembled as he considered it.

"I'll be right here," she said by way of reassurance, but there was nothing she could do for him while he was inside.

"Your drinks," the waitress said, causing Moss's heart to flutter again as she brushed him with a breast accidentally-on-purpose while setting down the drinks.

"Nice try, but it's me that's tipping," Sandra told the girl with a snort.

Disappointment washed over the waitress's face and she left the table without saying another word.

Moss stared at the yellow drink in the plastic coconut before him. He didn't want to go in. He knew that better than he knew anything. But he also knew his grandmother was correct. They had bounty hunters to pay and he needed Patchwork to look at the program.

"Fine," he said, lifting the drink and sucking as much as he could through the straw. "I'll do it."

CHAPTER 7

It had taken Moss a while to get into the program. His trepidation had kept his brain from allowing him to enter. But after another drink and relentless cajoling from his grandmother, he had opened his eyes in the program in his mind.

But this time, he was not in his hex. He saw a green blur before the world came into focus.

It was moss; he was surrounded by moss. The program told his brain he was smelling wet air suffused with plant life, dirt and mulch. A small stream bisected the space. Mounds of earth and rocks were covered in low leafy greens. Glass walls surrounded him, and a light fog enveloped him. He knew the space. The little room in The Conservation where the scientists were housing the plant for a future that might never come.

"Fuck," he said. He had always been in his hex in the program, always had access to a computer. This was different and it made him more worried than he already was. Every time he accessed this program, it became more complicated.

He felt a warm breeze on his body and looked down to see his naked form, pale and thin with the new musculature of an active life. But it was also him as he used to be, fully human without any cybernetics. In reality, they were nearly invisible to the naked eye, but he could sense that he didn't have them here.

His heart rate increased as he frantically looked around, trying to will a computer into being. He pressed his eyes closed and tried to envision a screen but when he opened them, there was nothing but green. He began to fear that he would not only be unable to access the information from the booth, but that he could be trapped in the program.

"Hello, Moss," he heard two female voices say in eerie unison.

He turned and his mouth fell open. He recognized the Butler twins instantly. They had been famed throughout the burb for their matching beauty and now they stood before him as naked as he was. One blonde, one strawberry blond, both perfect in form. His hands broke into a sweat and the fact that he was in a program fell away for a moment. He couldn't help but stare at them, feeling his body stir with excitement.

The waitress had gotten to him and his arousal was fusing with the corrupting program. Their matching green, glistening eyes pierced him. His breaths came out in short, ragged bursts.

"Is this what you want?" one of them asked, swaying her hips, and pulling her arms back to accentuate her unrealistically perfect breasts. It had been so long, and his mind was such a fog, that he could not remember her first name. Nor her sister's.

"Or is this?" A man's voice.

He turned to see Stan smiling at him. His Adonis-like figure glowed in the light of an unseen sun. The 100% BEEF tattoo on his broad chest seemed to glisten and his massive penis began to grow before Moss's eyes.

Moss turned away and felt his heart lurch as he remembered the man dying in Carcer City. The memory was stuck in his mind. Stan had been his mentor and a friend when he needed one. The man had died for their cause and for Moss, and the guilt began to crush his mind.

Moss closed his eyes once more.

He hated this program. Hated his grandmother for making him go back in. Hated himself not being able to control it.

"Is it this?" He knew as soon as he heard the English accent. Forcing his eyes open, he saw Irene. Standing before him as she had in his room above her shop. Images of her limp body began to flood his mind. She gazed at him, but he could not shake the vision of her death.

There had been so much death.

He tried to remember the rooftop party and all the people they had helped as Irene stepped toward him and smiled before a single drop of blood rolled down her cheek like a tear.

"I'm sorry," he found himself saying, but the words evaporated into the ether. He wanted to vomit. He pressed his hands to his ears but the next words still pierced his mind.

"No," he heard Izzy say. "It's always been me."

The others were gone.

Izzy stood before him in her BurbSec armor with her arms folded in front of her chest. "It's always been me and you tased me and left me."

Her chestnut eyes lanced him with a look of disgust. Cold sweat poured down his body and his heart beat so hard he felt like he might collapse. He felt the guilt he had been carrying gnaw at him.

This was his truth.

He had known it. She had been upset with him and told him so, but his own guilt was the thing which defined their relationship.

She may have moved on, but he had not.

"I'm sorry," he said again.

"Get over it," she said with a light chuckle. She was a perfect memory, exactly as Moss imagined her. "Seriously, Moss," she said, stepping forward and putting a hand on his arm. He reached out and put one of his hands on top of hers. The armor was cold and hard. "You have to let this go. You made a mistake. You cannot let it dominate you. You cannot let all the mistakes, all the injustices, wounds and regrets keep you from acting. You need to turn the fucking page, man."

"You are just me," Moss said, his frustration clear in his words.

"Yeah, so what?"

"So this isn't actually helpful," Moss replied in annoyance. "I need to make things right with the real you. I don't need advice from my own brain. It's pointless."

"Is it?" she asked, cocking an eyebrow. "You clearly need to hear this or I wouldn't be here."

"No, you are here because this fucking program is breaking and my mind along with it," he said, letting the anger out. "That fucking waitress had her tits out and now I'm all muddled and my fucking grandmother should not have sent me back in here.

"I don't need advice from you; I just need to get to a computer!"

Izzy shook her head as though he was a foolish little kid. "You just keep telling yourself that."

"Now what the fuck does that mean?" he shrieked. "If you are just a part of me, does my subconscious know something I don't? Is there information I can't access? Tell me!"

"Pathetic," she said but her voice was not her own. It was that of Warden Ninety-Nine. He felt a fist close around his neck and blinked.

Izzy was gone.

The moss was gone.

The Warden had him by the neck, lifting him off the ground. He was somewhere he had never been — an imagined prisoner holding cell similar to, but not the same as, those in Carcer City. As in a dream, it wasn't accurate to life.

Where there would have been lightbulbs, there were torches. The bricks of the walls were hexagonal and there was no floor; just pitch blackness.

Moss kicked against the black-clad figure. It was just like Carcer officer armor, but the material was metal and chain. The dark knight tightened his grip as Moss tried to pull at its wrists to no avail.

"I have you now." A voice came from inside the dark helmet. Moss knew the voice but couldn't place it. It was threatening and ominous and he felt his consciousness fading.

He wondered if he had died within the program, if he would in die real life as well. He wondered if his grandmother was holding his body as it thrashed around the bar.

He gasped but no air came. The world grew dark. The torches became little dots of orange dancing in the gloom.

He gasped, feeling air fill his lungs once more.

The light of his hex made him blink the world into focus.

He was lying in his bed.

He couldn't move; his body would not obey his mind. He lay there, thinking of all the images, all the things he had just seen and felt.

He had never experienced a lucid dream but imagined it was like that.

"I'm really fucking broken," he said to himself. It wasn't just the program, but himself. He had not given himself any time to process all the things he had gone through and they were now crushing his mind. Even how much his dedication was wavering was emblematic of his fractured brain.

He pondered, curious if it wasn't the program that was breaking, but him.

He exhaled slowly and stood. He didn't know why, but when he stretched it felt good. Exhausted, he plopped down in the ergonomic chair at his workstation and opened his computer display.

He considered calling Izzy, trying to reach her one more time, but thought better of it. He had to go see her, speak to her and finally get it all out.

Sighing, he stared at the projected screen and didn't move.

He felt a slight smile cross his lips. He knew how much was at stake and how much needed to be done quickly. But until he interacted with the outside world, time was all but paused.

He couldn't help himself. Rather than getting straight to work, he selected the music player and let Beethoven fill the room. He let the music course through him and take his mind from all his worries.

Moving in a near dance, he glided over to the shower, pressed his preferred setting button and stepped in. The hot water cascaded over him. It didn't matter that it wasn't real; it felt good. All the showers in all the safe houses were the same: cramped, dingy and miserable. Bugs slithered out from behind peeling tiles, one flickering lightbulb illuminated the space poorly, the cracked smart mirror displayed error messages and the one available towel was always, eternally damp.

Moss smiled as the hex filled with steam and he stepped from the space feeling like a new man. He didn't bother dressing and sat back down at the computer display.

He began to work his way through the program. His mother had designed it to be easy and he found simple drop-down menus.

SECURITY >

LOCAL >

GNUBS' EMPORIUM >

SEARCH

He entered "Corp's Bane" and the screen filled with lines of code he didn't understand as the program hacked for him. Once again, he was awestruck by his mother.

The inventory came up for the item. How much Gnubs had paid, how much she had marked it up and a video. He clicked through to the video and saw Patchwork, clear as day, approaching the booth. Shot from a camera mounted on a pole above the shop, Moss watched the scene unfold as his friend excitedly paid for the weapon.

Gnubs pulled out the long sword wrapped in burlap and began to untie the strings to reveal the weapon, and Moss understood what had happened.

In horror, he watched as three people, clad in dirty jeans, heavy boots and unmistakable leather vests, caught sight of Patchwork. One of them seemed to recognize him and began pointing and tapping the others. The thugs were dirty and tough looking, coated in tattoos with threatening spikes and chains adorning their outfits. In the parts of the city where Carcer offered no protection, the motorcycle clubs were the law.

Patch didn't notice anything as the three came up behind him. He seemed so happy to have found the sword that he was beaming ear to ear when one came up and slapped him on the back of the head. Patch wheeled around, hands raised in defense. He was always willing to help in a fight from behind a screen and had handled himself in real scraps, but he was hopelessly outnumbered and caught unawares.

Moss couldn't hear what the members of The Legion MC were saying, but their tone was obvious though their body language. Moss knew this whole thing was because of him. When he first arrived in the city, he had tased a Legion member and when he had first met Patchwork, they had worked together to take down many members of the gang.

They remembered, and it wasn't long before one took a swing at Patchwork. The young man fell to the ground in an instant and a huge bruiser of a woman picked him up and slung him over her shoulder.

The one who had cold-cocked Patch threw a cash chip at Gnubs before they took Patchwork out of sight. For a moment, Moss felt the all too familiar guilt but it quickly turned to anger.

It wasn't his fault.

The whole conflict with The Legion was because *they* had jumped him as soon as he arrived in the city. They had attacked him. They had now kidnapped his friend.

The relaxation induced by the shower was gone, replaced by a burning rage.

These gangs ran the streets because no one could stand up to them. There was no organized force that could fight back or cared to. Moss would get his friend back and change that. His cause was noble. He knew it. The citizens of the city should not have to live in constant fear because they couldn't afford justice.

He balled his fist, closed his eyes and willed himself back into the world.

CHAPTER 8

It didn't take long for his eyes to open. Moss felt his face pressed against his arm resting on the table. His nose filled with the scent of fruity cocktails.

"Welcome back," Sandra said, and before he could ask, she added, "you were only out a few minutes."

"The Legion has Patchwork and that shop owner let him get taken," Moss growled.

An evil grin crossed his grandmother's lips. "I have a contact in the Legion we can speak to, but would you like to chat with Gnubs on the way?"

Moss didn't have to consider it. "Yes, I would."

"Good," his grandmother said. "You don't always have to be good to do good."

Moss nodded. He had come to understand that truth. More and more, he had realized that changing the world was ugly and brutal. He had done things the kid in the hex would never have thought possible. He had stolen, taken revenge and killed more people than he could count.

He knew what they planned to do now was not about changing the world, but he didn't care. He was tired of bad people being allowed to be bad and wanted to make one small dent.

They strode back up to Gnubs' counter. The old woman scowled.

"Thought I made myself clear," she announced as they approached.

"You did," Sandra said with an icy voice. "Now we will make ourselves clear."

"Give us the Corp's Bane," Moss said, and his tone matched that of his grandmother.

"What wares I have is none of your concern," Gnubs seethed.

"Give it," Sandra reiterated.

Gnubs slammed her hands on the counter. "Get out of here!"

In a flash, Sandra's blade was out and she plunged it into the woman's left hand, securing it to the counter. The woman didn't scream or cry out. Moss assumed she had known pain her whole life.

"That was a mistake," she said, blood seeping from her hand.

"You gonna call yer friends at The Legion?" Sandra asked, wearing a clever smile. The comment seemed to take Gnubs by surprise.

"Just give us the fucking sword," Moss said through gritted teeth.

Gnubs reached under the counter with her free hand and produced the burlap wrapped weapon. Moss was happy he would be able to give his friend something nice — assuming he was alive.

Moss took the package. "Nice doing business with you."

"You'll pay for this," Gnubs said.

Sandra chuckled. "No, we won't," she said, and pulled the blade, rotated it and jammed it into the woman's throat. Gnubs gurgled and Moss dropped the sword bundle which fell to the ground with a low thud.

"What the fuck?" Moss shouted, glancing around to see a few people who had been watching look away quickly before scurrying away.

Sandra pulled the body toward the bars above the counter and reached in, pulling a keycard off the woman's neck. She hustled around the side and unlocked the door, calling to Moss.

He was still petrified. He had known they would threaten and hurt her but he had not expected the killing. His grandmother had always been pragmatic, and this was a surprise.

"Help me grab some shit," Sandra ordered.

Moss looked around again, knowing they were being watched. They were already outlaws, but this would certainly put them on even more radars. He ran in and began grabbing stuff at random, putting it in bags lying in a pile on the floor.

"Why?" he asked.

"Because she was a mouthy cunt and we could always use more supplies," Sandra said, as though the answer was obvious.

"People won't like it." Moss threw one bag over his shoulder and began to fill another one.

She scoffed. "What people? Carcer? The Legion? Got news for you, kid. They already want to see us hang."

She was right about that, but Moss was still troubled. Blood from the old woman's body began to coat the floor, and he told his grandmother it was time to go.

He stared out the window as they drove toward some bar Moss had already forgotten the name of. They seemed to drive past the same street over and over. The same shops, bars, liquor stores, people. A seemingly endless sea of destitution and misery.

"Patch *needs* to be okay," he said in a whisper.

"I know."

"No. You don't."

Sandra didn't speak again, allowing the space to fill with the sound of the engine and the world passing by.

"This program is breaking me," he said. "Or I'm breaking it. I don't even know anymore. My mind is a confused mess. I feel like a soup, just a liquid bag of emotions and digital input."

"Quite the picture you just painted." Although she was trying to hide it, Moss knew she was upset. He knew she loved him and wanted to protect him. He saw the hurt in her eyes as the lights of the city streamed across her face. "We will get him back and he will figure out what's going on."

"I hope so," he said. "To both. You should have seen them … I can't even imagine what they are doing to him now."

"Nothing good," Sandra said bluntly. "But we'll sort it."

Moss went back to staring, lost in his thoughts, until they pulled up to the Daughter of Thor's Son bar. An obese, leathered and grizzled man sat on the steps. He was sucking on a cigarette and had a cracked glass of beer beside him.

Moss could smell him as soon as they stepped from the vehicle. Body odor, sweat, filth and alcohol radiated from him. The sour stench made Moss wrinkle his nose. The man looked up at them with one good eye and one immobile cybernetic implant. If it had ever been functional, those days were long past.

"Hey, Murph," Sandra greeted him, plucking the cigarette from his mouth and taking a drag. Moss winced.

"Sandy, you old so-and-so, how they hell are ya?" Murph asked before looking around for his beer. It took him a long time to track down the drink and when he lifted it to his lips, more spilled down his beard than went down his gullet.

"I'm all right. You still with Legion?" she asked.

He pulled his long, white, yellow-stained beard aside to reveal the Legion emblem on his vest. "They can't get rid of me that easy. I was running these streets when these kids was still in diapers."

"Don't have time for a 'kids these days,' chat, Murph," Sandra said, flicking the cigarette butt down the street where it met its many abandoned brothers.

"I know," Murph said, trying to stand but failing before coughing. "Prez has a message for you."

"Shit," Moss said.

"This him?" Murph asked. "Wunderkind? Not much to look at."

"You're enough to look at for the both of you," Sandra half-joked. "What's the message?"

Murph set down the glass hard, cracking it further and rummaged in his pockets until he found a small holoprojector and set it on the concrete. The face of the Legion MC's president appeared. Moss had seen her once before and she looked as mean and angry now as she did then.

"Fuckers," she began. "As you know, we have your little friend. Quid pro quo time."

Moss could feel his grandmother vibrating with anger as the woman kept speaking. "What I need is simple: pick up a package and bring it to me. You do that and you will be reunited with your friend."

The display disappeared.

"That's all there was?" Sandra snorted.

Murph nodded, pulling a rumpled paper from his pocket and handing it to Sandra.

"Sure as shit ain't gonna be as easy as she made it sound," Sandra noted to Moss.

Murph laughed before breaking into another cough. "Got that right."

"What do you know?" She turned cold eyes on her friend and Moss wondered what history these two shared.

Murph shook his head. "Know? Nothing. But if she's making you do something, no chance it's going to be an easy ask."

Sandra rubbed her face in exasperation. "That's what I just fucking said."

"Reiterating to reinforce your point." Murph shrugged and took another drink.

"Pleasure as always," Sandra said, her words laced with condescension. "Best watch your back if the president knows we're friends. This turns sidelong, they may want a punching bag."

Murph waved the comment away. "Let 'em send some prospects and see what happens."

Sandra knelt and locked eyes with Murph. "Seriously, watch yourself."

Murph reached into his vest and produced a classic double-barreled sawed-off shotgun. "I'm always ready."

With characteristic speed, Sandra reached for the barrel and disarmed her friend in a flash, pointing the weapon at him. Moss was always impressed with his aging grandmother's agility.

"Shells don't mean shit without wit," she said as a grim reminder.

He smiled, and Sandra and Moss heard the familiar click of a pistol hammer being pulled back. It was done for dramatic effect and it worked. Moss had no idea how Murph had pulled the weapon or when, but he was impressed that the misdirection had worked on both of them.

"I'm *always* ready," he repeated.

Sandra yielded an impressed smile and handed the shotgun back. Murph put his weapons away. "And anyway, I don't need to be all that ready. Old timers like me can't be knocked off without approval. Even a local chapter president couldn't bury me on a whim."

"Honor among thieves," Moss put in and Murph looked at him incredulously.

"Something like that." He turned to Sandra. "It was good seeing you."

"Why you always make it sound like we ain't gonna meet again?"

He smiled but there was a deep sadness in his eyes. "You and I both know why."

"It was good seeing you, too."

"What's the deal with him?" Moss asked as they drove toward the location on the note.

Sandra shrugged. "Not much to tell."

"He serve with you?" Moss had come to realize that most of the people in Sandra's circle were folks she knew from the war.

She shook her head. "Nah," she said. "He was a friend we made afterward, when we were setting all this up. Burn used Murph to get us things we needed in the early days. Ain't easy to start a revolution; we needed anyone we could get back then.

"Murph lost his wife in the war and was happy to help veterans. Plus, The Legion recruited a bunch of our old boys back in the day. One of them uneasy alliances."

"That changed?" Moss asked.

"Yep, once we had our footing, we came to realize the clubs were as much a blight on the city as the megas. Murph stayed a friend but we cut business ties right quick."

There was so much history Moss didn't know. He had been swept up in this cause but had never taken the time to learn about it.

"So, how did all this begin? I feel like there is so much I should know."

"One day, I'll tell you. For now, let's get to work."

They pulled up to a nondescript warehouse in a sea of nondescript warehouses. Long and tall with brick facades, all of them had rounded roofs and large curved windows. The one they parked in front of had lights on and a heavy sliding metal front door.

A drudge stood beside the door, not moving.

"We are here to pick up a package," Sandra told the machine.

"Standby," it said, holding up a metal hand. It went quiet a moment as it communicated with someone inside. "You match the description and may enter." It turned to slide open the door. A person would have struggled to move such heavy metal, but the machine was able to do it with ease.

"Office at the back," it told them as they stepped through the door. It quickly closed behind them.

"What is this place?" Moss asked as he looked around the massive room. People sat shoulder to shoulder at desks only as wide as the ancient computer monitors at which they stared. They were crammed into every available space and scaffolding had been used to add three further layers of bodies, all staring at screens. Moss could see social media sites on every glowing monitor.

A loud air conditioning system rumbled through the space, recycling the smell of continuously brewing coffee and cigarette smoke. Nasty as the reek was, it cooled the space that would have been unbearably hot otherwise.

Men and woman with severe expressions and either tasers or riding crops stalked up and down the rows, ensuring every person was working at every moment.

"Fucking troll farm," Sandra explained as she pulled him forward toward the second-floor office at the rear of the building.

Moss knew what internet trolls were but didn't understand what use a place like this would be. "I—" he began, but his grandmother cut him off.

"Misinformation," she said. "Thousands of dummy accounts making millions of false points."

"Why?" Moss murmured.

"Keeping the people confused or angry about bullshit keeps them complacent. The companies know if the citizenry is sitting at computers or playing with palmscreens and arguing with these accounts, they aren't taking to the streets or waking up to their realities."

Moss shook his head as he walked past row after row of lies and deceit. Dust sprinkled down as a supervisor stomped along a plank between scaffolds overhead. No one looked at them as they moved deeper into the building.

"Why do it?" Moss found himself whispering as he looked down at a young woman with a deep purple and yellow bruise on her neck.

"Money."

This was the reality of the world: brutalizing and thankless jobs, squeezed in like sardines, abused and overworked. All just for the paycheck. As they neared the office, Moss looked at a young man with perfectly styled hair, spiked just-so with great care. He had a fine silver watch that shimmered in the harsh light. Moss could smell the presumably expensive cologne before it was dissipated by the air conditioner.

Moss couldn't help but wonder about the young man's life, working this job just so he could buy himself nice items. These status symbols were obviously important to him and worth this life.

Moss was snapped back to reality as an incredibly muscular man in an ill-fitting suit met them at the bottom of the stairs. Tribal tattoos showed through his white button-up shirt and peeked out of his collar like grass in pavement cracks. An interlaced gold and silver chain dangled from his neck and a large bull ring dangled from his nose. The man was no manager; just an enforcer for The Legion assigned to make sure their operation ran smoothly. No doubt he was cracking skulls rather than having staff meetings.

"You here for the package?" he asked, looking at the two as though they were completely unqualified to do the job.

"Seems that way," Sandra said.

He snorted, shook his head, and turned to ascend the stairs to the office, his boots thudding along the metal. He opened the door with a key and guided them into a small office where a metal baseball bat leaned against the doorframe. Several screens sat on piles of yellowed paperwork and old pallets, each one displaying a news feed. Voices coming from the screens chattered over one another, angry rants mixing with chat shows and biased talking-heads of one sect or another. The walls were lined with ripped and aging posters of naked women in garages, locker rooms and offices, and the room reeked of recently smoked marijuana.

An elevator door was at the rear of the room and the man waved his hand in front of a keypad to call the elevator up. The room shook as it approached from somewhere in the bowels of the building.

"It's just downstairs," he told them, absently pulling at a callus on the palm of his hand. "You can grab it and bring your car around front."

"Just like that?" Sandra asked dubiously.

"Just like that," he affirmed. "Some interested parties might attempt to … interfere along the way."

There it was. That was what Moss had been waiting to hear. Though he had known it was coming, his stomach still churned. They would need to contact the others and make sure they were running interference. Anders could keep an eye on them from above while Ynna, Gibbs and Puck could help keep the 'interested parties' at bay.

The doors slid open and they stepped in. Wires dangled in the corner where a camera had been aggressively removed. The floor was sticky and smelled of fresh piss, the stench rising when the doors closed.

Moss still hated elevators.

They rode down in silence and the doors opened to a subterranean parking garage, half of which had been turned into a crude server farm. More legion members guarded this area without pretense, all dressed in their motorcycle club uniforms rather than work ones.

The man gestured and they followed, walking past rows of half-stripped cars to a wooden crate with holes drilled in the top and metal handles crudely attached to the sides. At the sound of their approaching footsteps, Moss's fears were confirmed.

"Get me out of here!" a hoarse voice shouted from inside.

CHAPTER 9

The man they had been following kicked the side of the box, leaving a scuff mark next to many others. Whoever the person was inside must have been pissing their captors off frequently.

"The fuck is this?" Sandra growled.

The man showed gold teeth in a grin. "The fuck you expect?"

"Just have your own people do this," Moss said, his stomach churning. "We are not human traffickers."

The man shrugged. "No one said you were. Just need you to take this box to the president."

"There is a person in this box." Moss pointed an accusatory finger.

The man just chuckled. "Look, I don't know who you are or why you have to do this and frankly, I don't give a shit. All I know is that *you* are in charge of the box from here. What's in the box is none of your concern. Get me?"

Moss opened his mouth to speak, but Sandra cut him off.

"We get you. Kid, go pull the car around," she told Moss, who wanted to object but didn't speak as his grandmother handed him the keys. He knew they needed Patchwork back but bringing a person in a box to undoubtedly be tortured made him sick. But if it meant his friend was no longer going to be tortured, he understood why Sandra was agreeing.

Two more bikers walked him through the lot to a roll-up door they opened for him. He stepped out into the street, wondering what kind of person he was.

Hustling over to the van, he got in, fired up the engine and pulled around the building to the parking lot entrance. His driving was improving, but not by much and backing into the lot was jerky, ugly and nauseating. The gang members did not hide their amusement, outright pointing and laughing.

He parked the van and hopped out, opening the rear doors and watching as two of the Legionnaires lifted the box. It shifted as the person inside thrashed and one of them put his mouth to an airhole and spit in.

"I'm gonna kill you!" the voice screamed from within.

Moss turned his gaze to his grandmother, who tried to reassure him with a look. He hoped she had a plan. Once the box was loaded up, the manager said "Good luck out there" with such a sadistic grin, it was obvious he expected them to be killed along the way. "Here's the address," he added, and handed Moss a slip of paper.

Sandra and Moss didn't reply. They simply got in their vehicle and took off. Moss entered the address into the nav as they pulled into the street.

When they were a few blocks away, Moss whispered so the man in the box couldn't hear, "What's the plan?"

"This is a setup, right?" Moss asked when Sandra didn't answer immediately, knowing the answer and looking for affirmation.

"Right," Sandra agreed. "Either way, we are going to deliver the package and get Patchwork."

Moss shook his head. "Wait, what?"

"I don't give a fuck who's in that box or why. I'm getting Jo her kid back and us what we need. This package is getting delivered one way or another so it may as well be us gets paid."

"No," Moss said. "All of that *does* matter."

"Why?" Sandra asked. Moss wondered if she was testing him.

"Because we are the good guys," he said without hesitation, stealing another glance at the box sliding around the back as they rounded a corner.

"Sooner you realize we are the gray guys, the better," Sandra told him.

"We may have to do bad to do good, but this is fucked," he said, climbing between the seats toward the box.

"Hey, who are you?" he asked the box.

"Fuck you!" he got in response.

"That's fair," Moss admitted. "Listen to me. We are being strong-armed into doing this delivery and we could help you, but we need to know who you are and why The Legion has you."

"Think I'm an idiot? I'm not telling you shit," the box said. "Let me out of here and maybe I'll trust you."

"Now you think *I'm* an idiot."

"Well, either you are a Legion asshole who thinks I can be fooled, or you actually are someone who got so mixed up with the gang that you have to move me. So either way, it's a good bet."

"You're making it real easy to just want to leave you in there," Moss said. He had an idea. "Just look through the air hole; you'll see we aren't Legion."

"Right, because people can't change clothes," the box scoffed. "Anyway, I'm blindfolded you—"

At that, Sandra slammed on the brakes, sending the box hurtling forward to slam against the back of the seats. Moss had grabbed one of the wall-mounted grips just in time but felt as if his arm had nearly been pulled from his socket.

"The kid's trying to help you, idiot," she snarled. "Listen good. We are taking you to the Legion now, and I don't know what they have planned for you but it sure as shit ain't good. Tell us who you are and maybe we can help you; but otherwise, your lot in life is about to get real fucking grim."

No sound filled the space save the low hum of the engine for a long while. "Fine," the box said. "I'm Mygdon, a Road Captain for the Hoplites."

The corner of Moss's lip turned up. "How'd they get you? What do they want?"

"No big story. Asshole coldcocked me outside a pickup," Mygdon said, sounding ashamed. "Woke up in this box. Guessing they want intel from me. Hoplites are making moves these days while The Legion is still just trying to recover."

"See," Sandra said to Moss. "Just some ganger, no need to feel guilty. Let's go drop this garbage off."

"Oh, fuck you!" Mygdon screamed.

"No," Moss said, and Sandra raised an eyebrow. He pulled a disk out, once again wishing he had a palmscreen, and contacted Seti through their neural network.

Seti, he said, *need you to look up the contact info for Powers and put us though on my disk here.*

Sure thing, she said, and after a moment the face of the gangster appeared as a projection in the car. The glow from the hologram reflected on all the walls and windows.

"Dobriy vecher," Powers said with a friendly smile. "It has been too long."

Moss had helped Powers solve a problem long ago and knew the man worked closely with the Hoplites. He looked well put together and cheerful. Being the most powerful man in a district clearly agreed with him.

"It has," Moss said, trying to be casual but still sounding frantic. Sandra crawled around into the back of the idling van as Moss explained the situation and what he had planned.

Powers listened and nodded along. "You will give us the location of the troll farm as well, yes?" he asked.

"Sure," Sandra interrupted, "so long as you put half of 'em to work for us."

Powers' lips curled into a knowing smile. "Certainly," he said. "Speak after."

He signed off. Moss and Sandra got back in their seats and she pulled back into the street.

"What was that?" Moss asked.

"We need to start rallying support," Sandra told him. "We have street teams out there, but we need to get our message out if we ever want to take this fight to the companies."

"I know, but there has to be a better way," Moss said. "Those poor people are the exact ones we want to help. Doesn't feel right to take advantage of them too. Then we are just as bad as the people we are fighting."

"We are not, because we aim to free those folks at the end. They're gonna be doing that job between now and then and they may as well be doing it for us."

That was the second time she had used that argument in the last few minutes and Moss was having a hard time coming up with a retort. "Still, it feels wrong."

"A lot of shit feels wrong," Sandra said. "That's why we are gonna fight until it feels good."

"Who are you people?" Mygdon asked from inside the box.

Moss smiled. "The people who just saved your life."

Moss could tell they were approaching The Legion's local base of operation by sound alone. Motorcycle engines revved and called to one another from every street and down every alley. Leathered gangers darkened every doorway and patronized every establishment. There were far fewer ads in this neighborhood. The screens, moving posters and projections were noticeably absent here.

Rather than looking like they were heading to some menial job, the people who crowded the streets appeared as though they were heading only to, or stumbling from, a bar. It wasn't long before the first motorcycle pulled up alongside them, roaring up to their right. The clubs preferred wheeled bikes. While any who could afford it used flighted vehicles, the gangs roamed on the streets, although they undoubtedly also had the flighted style in their stables as well.

"They're gonna be mighty suspicious that the Hoplites didn't get us," Sandra noted.

Moss sighed. He was relieved that Powers had been able to keep the Hoplites from harassing them along the route, but the next part would be trickier. "Maybe they won't notice."

"They will," Mygdon said, wiggling a finger through one of the air holes. "Whole point of making you do this was to either be killed by my friends or somehow survive and deliver me to them. Win-win for The Legion."

"No one asked you," Moss said, rubbing his palms across his face. "I liked you better as a box."

A second bike pulled up on the left and another at their rear. Moss took a deep breath as he watched the number of headlights grow like a swarm of fireflies. Every bike that rolled by joined the caravan. Moss didn't know whether their plan would work.

One more bike rumbled in front of the van, turning to guide it past a guard station flanked by tall walls. They approached a structure with a large parking area at the front. A classic brick building stood on the right with a taller, glass-fronted building growing from its side — clearly a later addition.

A Legion flag whipped in the wind above the buildings and four more gangers huddled under a cement awning. The words "Police Department" were etched into a low wall, covered in spray painted emblems and logos. This building had become derelict after the city switched over to the private police force.

Sandra brought the van to a stop, the bikers all pulling in around her and pointing their lights toward the arched door of the brick building.

She turned to Moss. "Plan best work."

Moss gave her a crooked smile. "Here's hoping."

They got out of the van, leaving the doors ajar, and stepped to the front as a few Legion members opened the back and pulled out the box. They lugged it around the van and plunked it down beside Moss and Sandra. Moss felt his hands go numb, as they so often did in critical moments.

The door to the building swung open. Out stepped the burly woman with the shaved head whom Moss had met once before in what felt like another life. She had a few new scars, but her eyes were as fierce and menacing as ever. The other bikers all made way for her as a sign of deference as she sauntered forward, the chains hanging from her pants jingling.

She wore thick brown boots with long, blood-covered spikes protruding from the toes. Her denim pants were stitched and reinforced with metal plates and her black leather vest was covered in patches representing her position and territory. The word "President" was displayed over her right breast.

"Survived the ride," the president said, shifting her weight and placing her left hand on a gun holstered at her hip.

Sandra smiled ominously. "Just lucky, I guess."

"You assholes are nothing but lucky," the president said in disgust.

The moment was tense. Moss knew she was disappointed that they had survived and he hoped she would just hand over Patchwork. He feared what shape his friend would be in, terrified about what they must have done to him.

"We brought your box," Sandra said, pointing. "Where's the boy?"

The president clicked her tongue. "No foreplay?"

"I don't intend to get fucked," Sandra growled. "Give us the kid and our business will be concluded.

At that, the president smiled and turned to a vicious-looking ganger to her right. "Bump, bring out the breaker."

The legionary looked right at Moss, flaring her mouth open to expose sharpened metal teeth before turning to retreat inside.

"You two have been stirring up trouble all over town," the president said, arching her back and causing her spine to crackle. "That's our job."

"There's enough trouble to go around," Sandra said. The tension was so thick in the air that Moss could hardly breathe.

The president nodded slowly. "Got that right. Doesn't mean I want to share."

Sandra put her hands up and cocked her head, trying to diffuse the moment. "Different goals."

The door opened and Bump walked out, Patchwork at her side, his voice filling the open space.

"Just tell her that you want to be friends," Patchwork was advising casually before turning. "Moss!" he called and came running over to hug him. Patch wasn't injured and didn't seem scared or under duress at all. "What the hell are you doing here?" he asked, pulling away but keeping his hands on Moss's arms.

Moss was so confused that it took him a moment to react. *Okay*, he thought. The gangers all began to laugh.

"We are here to rescue you."

Patchwork smiled. "That's cool. These guys took me in a while."

"We saw you get taken," Moss stammered.

Patchwork nodded, his dreadlocks bouncing. "Sure, sure," he said affably, seemingly unaware of the situation around him. "Things started out rocky since … well, you know, but once they saw my skills, they grew to love me. I mean, who doesn't, right?"

He beamed at the nonplussed Moss.

The president was still chuckling. "Thank you for my delivery," she said with a smug smile. "And as you can see, your friend remains unmolested."

"Molested?" Patchwork grimaced at the president. "Why you gotta use words like that, Beck?"

"Boss!" one of the gangers called from a tower built into the wall just before an alarm began to blare.

Moss grabbed Patchwork and threw him toward the door to the van as the sound of motorcycles thundering up the streets filled the air. Guns were pulled and wild shots sounded as the lid to the box flew open, splintering as the only nail they had left in place pried free. Mygdon raised Sandra's ankle gun and fired directly into the face of the president. Her look of shock froze in place as she was blasted back, sending confused cries through the space. The van was riddled with bullets though most of the legionaries were focused on the Hoplites pouring into the lot.

"What's happening?" Patchwork shouted as he and Moss cowered. A bullet smashed the door window above their heads.

"Didn't realize you'd make friends! Plan was already in motion!" Moss called as Patch leapt into the front of the van. Moss pulled his Kingfisher and fired a bolt into the back of a thug, sending him crashing to the ground.

"No!" Patchwork yelled, the color draining from his face as Sandra shot Bump through the heart, blood spraying into the night. Muzzle flash glowed in the smoke. More motorcycles arrived in a deafening roar, each one with a second Hoplite firing shots from the back of the seat or from a sidecar.

The few remaining legionaries began to fire skyward. Heat from the lowering dropship radiated around the van. Anders gave a wave from the cockpit and Ynna fired an SMG from each hand as she leapt from the ship down onto the roof of the van. Gibbs took precision shots from the side door. Steampuck slid down a rope and a gangster charged him desperately with a crowbar. Puck pulled an ornate scimitar from his side and cut so deep into his attackers' shoulder that it severed the spine.

He let out a throaty laugh. "Sixteenth century steel, mon frère."

Hoplites surrounded one remaining legionary, who pulled the trigger of her empty revolver hopelessly. She used her cybernetic left arm to throw her weapon at one of the approaching hoplites, striking him with such force that he was knocked to the ground. His brothers-in-arms laughed before helping him up.

One Hoplite pulled off her helmet and looked at the terrified Legion prospect. She wore nothing under her vest, held closed with a single button, and assless chaps out of which a slight thong could just be seen at the top. Moss wondered if her role was simply to be eye-candy.

"You run and tell your friends that we own the Wallburg *and* downtown now," the Hoplite leader told the girl. She looked for a moment as if she was going to take one last stand and die fighting, but instead she ran over to a bike and sped off.

The leader turned to Moss. "Thanks for the intel," he called out, and seeing a bloody but alive Mygdon clambering out of the box, added, "and for my brother."

"You can owe us one," Sandra called back over the sound of the ship landing beside the van, knocking it over and crushing motorcycles along the way. The head Hoplite nodded and Ynna strode over and gave Moss a congratulatory slap on the cheek before running to pull Patchwork from the van for a hug.

"I'm never letting you leave the safehouse again," Ynna told him with a smile. "Assuming Jo doesn't kill us all first."

"Oh, yeah," Patchwork smiled shakily. "Mom's gonna be pissssed."

"Patch," Gibbs said as he and Anders approached from the ship.

"Gibbs, Anders," Patchwork greeted. "Who's this dapperass dude?"

Everyone groaned as Puck bellowed, "I am Steampuck. Rogue, charlatan, miscreant, and all-around ne'er-do-well. Bastard, prick, and thorn in the side of all megas. Swashbuckler, venturer, and hero of the commoner."

Patchwork laughed as he shook the man's hand, but his face fell as he turned and looked at the carnage behind him. Wordlessly, he walked over and knelt by the body of Bump, whom he had been advising on relationships just a moment before. His eyes welled and he placed a hand on that of the body's. Shaking his head, he looked up at them miserably.

"Doesn't always have to be this way," he said. "Not that I'm ungrateful, but…"

"We didn't know," Moss said, feeling guilty even though he had just rescued his friend. He wondered if there might have been a different way, if they could have done this without the bloodshed.

"Sorry, kid, but we gotta clear out," Sandra said with her usual detachment. "Bodies'll be piled higher if we don't get you to your mom."

"Okay," he said, standing. Moss could tell he was taking this hard.

"You'll come with us after," Sandra informed Patch, and it wasn't a question.

"Sure," Patch agreed.

Gibbs came over and squeezed Moss on the shoulder. "We have a surprise for you."

CHAPTER 10

Silence reigned in the ship for the entire ride to the saloon, where they dropped off Patchwork with the understanding that he would meet them after reuniting with his mom. He thanked them profusely when they left, but Moss could tell that his friend's head was still swimming. Sandra had stayed behind to make sure that he made it back to them unscathed and to undoubtedly rub her success in Jo's face.

As soon as he was out of the van, Moss turned to Gibbs. "So, what's the surprise?"

Gibbs rolled his eyes and Ynna butt in, "It wouldn't be one if we told you, dipshit."

"Ugh, fine," Moss said, unable to fathom what they could be talking about. "Maybe you could just tell me—" but Gibbs started speaking, intentionally burying Moss's words.

"You know what I've always wondered?"

"What's that?" Ynna said, playing along with a bemused smirk.

Moss sighed and Gibbs continued. "Who sets up our safehouses? I mean, we always show up and they are mostly completed. Do little elves scout locations and set everything up?"

Ynna shook her head. "No, we have a crew whose job is finding places and setting them up for the various teams. Shit, Gibbs, you even met the girl who wired us for the game the other month."

"Oh, yeah," he said, thinking back.

Their banter was not amusing Moss so much this time as he tried to figure out what they could have up their sleeves.

"A kid named Tek set up the place we are currently in," Ynna explained. "Nothing just happens. When Burn died, I had to step up and take on a lot of the minutia that would have been missed otherwise. Seti is helpful, but it's a lot of legwork for me."

"That could be a cool game," Gibbs said, looking out the window to the city below.

Ynna cocked an eyebrow, seeming a little perturbed that no one thanked her for the work she had just mentioned. "What could?"

"A rebel safehouse sim," he said, obviously starting to think of how it would work.

Ynna chuckled. "Well, you can go into game design once we change the world."

"I suppose we will have other priorities when that happens," Gibbs sighed.

Anders held up the ship a moment before they proceeded to the safehouse. "Got to take a minute to scan, cloak and make sure we weren't followed."

They waited as Gibbs continued to explain his idea for the game. The ship started to move again, and they landed on the roof of the abandoned building they had been using, pulling forward under a chunk of half collapsed floor so the ship wouldn't be visible from drone scans.

They all stepped out and Puck said, "I'll stay here with Anders and help him tarp and cover this contraption."

Anders nodded his thanks and Ynna mocked playfully, "Contraption."

They pulled open the heavy firedoor leading to the roof and Moss shot Gibbs a questioning look.

"Your room," his friend said, unable to hide his grin.

Moss had an inkling of what it could be but didn't want to get his hopes up. Nearly running to the room, he opened the door cautiously and didn't see anything at first. But at the sound, a form shifted on his bed.

Moss's heart nearly leapt from his chest and he had to grip a lamp to keep from collapsing. The sound of the lamp shade falling to the ground roused her fully and Issy looked up at him, her unkempt black hair falling into her face before she brushed it behind her ears.

She smiled, jumped up and darted over to hug him. Moss was so exhausted from the two gun battles and recovery in between that she knocked him into the wall.

He didn't care. He was more excited to see her than he had ever been to see anyone.

"You're here," he managed to gasp, and she pulled out of the hug, turning her big brown eyes on his as they began to well.

"I'm here," she assured him.

More than all the feelings he harbored for her, he was happy to see one of his oldest friends. Of course, she was still as beautiful to him as ever. She wore a patterned yellow dress with green flowers stitched throughout, black leggings and a red scarf bundled around her neck and cascading down her shoulders.

The version of her in the program was always generated with computerized flawlessness but he preferred the way she looked in real life. He loved her slightly upturned nose, eyebrows showing where she had plucked and somewhat cracked lips from an overreliance on balm.

"I'm sorry," he found himself saying. "For so much."

"I know," she nodded. "But I'm done with simple apologies and awkward conversations. We are going to talk now. Talk about it all. We have to. I could lose you at any moment and I'm over leaving things unsaid. There is too much here, there has always been so much, and we can't jeopardize that over discomfort."

Moss's heart smiled and his face followed. He had wanted to do this for so long but hadn't been able to muster the courage. He had convinced himself that it was a matter of not having time, but he had always known it had just been fear. As she had so often in their lives, she had stepped up again now.

She took him by the hand and pulled him down to sit beside her on the bed.

"So, what are you sorry for?" she asked with a bluntness he had missed.

"So many things," he said.

She smiled but shook her head. "Not an answer."

After a moment, he said, "I'm sorry I shot you and left you. I should never have done that."

She nodded in agreement. "You shouldn't have, but that also shouldn't be what you are sorry for."

"No?" he asked, and it felt like old times. She had always been the one to teach him how to better deal with people. Though so much had changed, in this moment they might as well have been kids back in his hex.

"No," she stated. "You should be sorry for not trusting me. You thought I had betrayed you, thought I would have chosen my job over you. Shooting me was not great but doubting me was worse. I have been there for you every day of your life. I sat with you, cried with you, cared for you when your parents disappeared. I defended you when Gibby would bust your chops. I asked that girl to dance with you when you were too shy to do it yourself. I was by your side for everything and when you shot me, it wasn't the blast that hurt." She paused, letting her words sink in before winking. "I mean, the blast hurt too."

"I know, I should never have doubted you," he said. "I won't try to excuse my behavior, but you must understand that I was thrown pretty quickly into some serious shit and I didn't even really know what was happening. Nothing was what I had thought and so I made a mistake I'll never be able to take back."

"I knew that even at the time," she said. "But in all that confusion, I should have been the one thing you knew you could count on. I always have been and I always will be."

"This is one of those things that you have to know: that in my heart, I really do know. And I hope you never doubt it. I know I shot you and I fucked up, but I'll really always be here for you." He plucked up a piece of his blanket and rubbed it between thumb and forefinger. He wondered if he was even making sense anymore, but if there was anyone who would understand, it was Issy.

"I know you believe that in this moment," she said, a slight sullenness in her tone. "I just wish you could have believed it in the heat of the moment as well, you know?"

"Yeah." He understood what she meant. He was guilty and miserable for hurting her, but he was happy to finally be having the conversation. Issy was finally airing her grievances so that hopefully they could move on together.

"You had a relief aide of me," she said, not breaking eye contact. Moss wished she had said anything else, but he knew it was time to get this over with. He had long assumed she had known, but now he knew for sure and had to pay the price.

"Um, so here's the thing, it's just, well, here, what you have to understand is," but the words weren't coming. He didn't know what to say, what to tell her.

"So," she said, putting her hands on her hips. "How was she?"

Moss felt his mouth fall open.

Issy rolled her eyes, laughed and shoved Moss on the shoulder. "I'm just messing with you," she chuckled. "It's gross *and* I don't care how it was."

"Oh," he said. "So, what do you care about?"

She scrunched her face, looking as amused as she was annoyed by his confusion. "What do you think?"

"I think questions like that are a trap," he said honestly.

"I know, right?" Issy smiled. "We girls really are just the worst."

"I mean, you have to be upset that I had sex with a robot I paid to have look like you," Moss said after a long pause.

She dropped her head and snorted. "Yeah, that's not great, but the act isn't what bothered me."

"Really?" he asked, genuinely confused. For all his instincts in combat and desperate situations, Moss was still a novice when it came to matters of the heart and he knew it.

"Yeah, really," Issy said. "You went that route without even bothering to ask me out. You aren't Gibbs, that isn't you. The man I know would have at least tried to get the real thing before resorting to a machine."

"I was drunk," he justified, more to himself than to her.

"Yeah, yeah," she chided. "You may have been when you hired the aide, but you weren't all the time we were together."

She had him there. Moss paused a moment, staring at a long crack in the drywall opposite him as though it might hold some answers. He asked himself why he hadn't asked her out. He had wanted to, and came close so many times, but he had never pulled the trigger. He had convinced himself that he didn't want to jeopardize their relationship, but looking back now, he understood that he had just been scared — scared of rejection or that she might see him differently.

"It's true," he admitted.

"Why didn't you just ask me out if that's what you wanted?" she pressed gently, putting her hand on his face to turn him to her. "Is that what you wanted?"

There it was — the question he had feared for as long as he had known the answer. He stared into those beautiful eyes that had been with him for his whole life. He knew the answer, knew what he needed to tell her.

"Yes," he said and before she had time to speak, he added, "Would you have dinner with me?"

She smiled and let out a sigh of relief. "Yes, of course. Yes."

He couldn't believe it. A weight that had been sitting on him since he was thirteen lifted for the first time.

She took his hand in hers. "Took you long enough."

"Guess I was waiting for the right moment," he joked at his own expense. "How did you find out? About the relief aide? Gibbs tell you?"

She shook her head and laced her fingers through his. "No, worse."

He had guessed at the alternative but was mortified to think it was true.

"I was working the security office and Clam called me over. I didn't think much of it because he was always showing me dumb videos, but I was shocked when I saw that I was wearing a slutty dress and going into your room.".

His heart sank. "I'm sorry you had to see that and that you had to see it with someone."

"Me too," Issy said. "But that wasn't the worst part. Can I level with you?"

"Always," Moss told her, squeezing her hand tenderly.

She looked away for the first time and Moss saw her cheeks redden slightly. "I had suspected how you felt for a long time, years really. I had just been waiting. Waiting and waiting and waiting.

"I just didn't get it. And then I started to get into my own head, started to doubt if you really did have feelings for me. Because..." she trailed off and Moss watched her, her eyes a million miles away. "Because I wanted you to like me."

The moment hung between them before she continued. "You may have been pining for me, but what you clearly didn't understand was that it was a two-way street. You had always been there for me too. You supported me when I wanted to join BurbSec, worked and studied with me. You were there when my mom moved out and you made me tough. Remember when Stephanie Bauch kept pushing me and being mean?"

"Vaguely," Moss admitted.

"Well, I do. I came to you thinking that you would do some boy thing and defend my honor. You remember what you did?"

Moss smiled, remembering now. "I told you to confront her and tell her to stop."

"Right," Issy said. "You didn't try to take my power, you told me to use it. I think that was part of the reason I wanted to join BurbSec. You helped me to understand that I never had to be weak. It was the moment ... the moment I..." she didn't have to finish the sentence.

Moss wrapped his hand around her head and pulled her forward gently. He heard her breath catch just before their lips met. Butterflies didn't begin to express how Moss felt in that moment. It was more like the fireworks show at D2Eland going off in his chest.

The fight, the bullet wounds, the program, all of it was forgotten. Her warmth, spirit and love were all he felt. He didn't know how long they had been kissing when she finally pulled away.

She was beet red and beaming but said, "That was lovely, but I still have a lot of unresolved stuff, so let's still do dinner."

"That would be perfect," Moss said. "When?"

"Tomorrow night? I think we will be busy tonight."

"We will?"

"That's the other thing I wanted to talk to you about," she said, gesturing to a duffel bag next to the door that Moss hadn't even noticed.

"Really?" he asked, unable to mask his excitement.

Issy simply nodded. "Gibbs has been clearing out one of the rooms for me."

Moss chuckled, understanding now why his friend had been asking about the people who set up safehouses. "What changed?"

Issy shook her head as if trying to cast off a difficult memory. "I just got back from Seattle. I was there for my aunt's funeral."

"I'm so sorry," he said.

"She was killed by Carcer." The mood in the room changed immediately. "She was walking her dog in a nice part of the city while my uncle was at the optometrist. Her dog barked at some rich bitch. She apologized, but the woman, this horrible, vile creature, put a bounty on her. When Carcer came to pick her up, she talked back and…"

That was all she could say, her red eyes beginning to tear. Moss enveloped her. "I'm so sorry," he repeated. His heart broke for his friend, but also for a world where this kind of story was the reality. Where the rich could do anything they wanted and everyone else was left out in the cold —or worse.

"Dad told me it was time, and I knew he was right," she murmured. "He says 'hi,' by the way."

Moss smiled and Issy continued. "I knew I couldn't just make Korma anymore. The same thing that drove me to join BurbSec made me come here. I need to be a part of something, to help people. This world is rife with pain and misery and I'm lucky enough to know some people trying to change that. So here I am. Here to help, here to fight."

"I can't even tell you how much I needed that right now," Moss said, the sentence like a release valve for pent-up feelings.

"Really?" Issy asked. "One of the big leaders of a global revolt needs little old me?"

Moss chuckled. "I've been struggling. In a lot of ways, but also in wondering if what I'm doing is important. One minute, I feel like it's what I was born to do and the next I can hardly justify any of it. Hearing your story, knowing you are here and want to be, is more inspiring than all the speeches my grandmother could give me."

Issy just smiled at him for a moment. "She is quite something from what I keep hearing."

"Grandma? Yeah, she takes some warming up to."

"I always wondered where you got that little badass streak. I guess I'll see soon."

"Oh, yes."

"Anything I can do to ingratiate myself?" Issy asked. "This is the most bizarro meeting-the-family ever."

"Just be you," Moss said. "It's bullshit she hates worse than anything."

"Okay," Issy said. "So, what's been going on?"

Moss thought for a moment before answering. He was happy now, comforted. The talk had been short but what he had needed for so long. He knew there would be more to work through and that his apologies wouldn't be enough but he was, for the moment, happy.

CHAPTER 11

It had been morning when they had arrived back and late morning by the time Issy finally left Moss alone in his room. As soon as she had, his head hit the pillow and he slept like death until a light knock struck the wall next to his open door.

Gibbs grinned as he walked in, the smell of the coffee he was holding reaching Moss before his eyes even adjusted.

"Thanks," Moss said, sitting up in bed and taking the warm mug. "And not for this."

Gibbs smirked. "Well, I mean, you *could* thank me for the coffee too."

"How about, thanks for everything," Moss said and took a sip, allowing the heat of the drink to spread throughout his body.

"Happy to do it," Gibbs said. "Issy seemed pretty bummed when she got here but was nearly skipping when she left your room."

"We finally talked," Moss told his friend.

"I'm happy for you," Gibbs said. "And me! I'm always stuck gaming with Ynna and she always kicks my ass, so it'll be nice to have Issy to play with."

Moss chuckled. "Issy always kicked our asses too."

Gibbs pointed and winked. "Yes, but not by as much. Anyway, we are going to meet over dinner. Issy cooked."

"*That's* why it finally smells good in here."

Gibbs pouted. "I'm still learning all right? And I don't see you cooking for everyone."

"Well, I'm very busy and important," Moss said, trying to hold back a laugh. "Hero of the rebellion and all."

"Oh, yes, all that getting captured and shot at is really sticking it to them," Gibbs joked.

Moss smiled as Gibbs helped him to his feet. "You really have been hanging around Ynna too much. Quips like that are actually clever."

"I'm learning," Gibbs said sheepishly. "You know, I'm really starting to love her."

Moss outright laughed. "Yeah, no shit. Coolest chick you've ever met is willing to sleep with you? Of course you're in love with her."

Gibbs dropped his head. "She really is out of my league, though."

Moss put a hand on his friend's shoulder. "No, Gibbs, she isn't. You two are actually a perfect match."

"You really think so?" Gibbs asked as he stared down at his left hand, tucked into his jacket pocket.

Moss cocked his head. "I do." Gibbs didn't say anything and Moss took a slow sip of his coffee. "Whatcha got there?" he asked playfully, thinking he knew the answer.

Gibbs flushed, realizing he had been caught. "Nothing."

"Don't make me come over there."

"It's," Gibbs said in a whisper, "this."

He held out a small, blue, velvet-covered box. Moss knew instantly. "Well, no shit?"

"Don't know when or even if I'll offer it, but I guess I wanted to be ready," Gibbs murmured. "I know it's maybe too soon, but our life expectancy is…" he didn't have to finish the thought.

"Think she'll want it?" Moss asked.

"From me? No idea," Gibbs admitted. "But in general, yes."

"Really?" Moss asked, more than a little surprised.

Gibbs chuckled. "That's the thing. Everyone sees her as this badass, but that's not all she is. Being tough in the sorta traditional macho sense doesn't make her any less of a woman. She can still love frilly shit and looking pretty *and* beat the snot out of some biker, you know?"

Moss was amazed by his friend. He had grown so much. He might still quote movies and want to play video games all day, but he was smart and understanding and saw things in a way Moss felt he was still learning.

"You're right," Moss said and beamed at his friend. "You're the best man I know and you guys are perfect for each other."

"Not as perfect as you and Issy," Gibbs said quietly, deflecting.

"I don't need to tell you how complicated that is," Moss said.

Gibbs laughed through his nose. "No, no you do not."

They were silent for a moment.

"Okay," Gibbs said. "Get showered and changed. You smell like a gunpowder factory."

"Not your best work."

"Yeah, it didn't feel great as I said it," Gibbs smiled. "Guess I need to spend more time with Ynna."

"You do that," Moss said, setting the coffee on the floor, since the room had no furnishings save the bed and a pile of clothes.

Gibbs left and Moss made his way to the shower, no longer caring how shitty the real thing was.

He threw on some black jeans and a gray shirt after the shower and walked down the hallway of exposed rotting wood and peeling wallpaper to a sound he had rarely heard in the building. Laughter. He saw plates heaped with rice, curry and meat set on a broad table held together with rusted screws and zip ties, and under an old chandelier poised to crash out of the ceiling at any moment.

"Moss!" everyone cried as though they hadn't seen him in ages. He saw an empty chair between Issy and Gibbs and sat down, instantly picking up the bent spoon and shoveling food into his mouth. Ynna fed Perro a scrap and gave the little dog a scratch behind the ear.

"You did all that in the game?" Issy asked.

Ynna laughed. "Yeah. We were just there to find Judy, but it became something bigger."

"Freedom fighters through and through," Judy said.

"Time to get down to business," Sandra announced. "Judy rigged the tech with Patchwork's help, so we have work to do."

Issy raised her hand, bringing a chorus of laughter from the group.

"Yes?" Sandra asked, and even she was wearing a smile.

"I've been gone a minute. Can someone catch me up?" Issy asked.

All eyes turned to Moss. "Where to begin?" he said, gulping down another mouthful.

"Okay," Gibbs cut in with a grin. "Here's a quick recap: Moss's parents were killed by ThutoCo because Moss's dad had created a personality mapping program that was going to be misused by the company. He began feeding information to his mother," Gibbs pointed to Sandra, who grimaced, "and her lover, Burn. Moss's dad gave Moss a way to destroy the program which could only be unlocked when he was old enough. What he didn't know was that his wife had added to the program to make it much more useful for hacking.

"With your help, we destroyed all the research, though it seems that ThutoCo has recovered much of the data. They were pissed, as was Carcer, and some of our crew were arrested. We broke into Carcer City to rescue our friends as well as Sandra.

"While we were escaping, Moss got caught and taken to a holding facility in South Africa where Carcer hoped to break into his brain to grab the program Moss's family put there. Turns out everyone wants it. Following so far?"

Issy nodded slowly, her eyes wide. She had heard bits and pieces of this, Moss knew, but hadn't had the whole thing laid out. Moss hadn't really taken the time to think about everything he had been through and was enjoying the story, though Gibbs was glossing over huge and painful portions.

Gibbs pointed to Steampuck. "With the help of a new friend, Moss escaped from Carcer and we discovered they were going to unveil some new technology. We flew to meet Moss in Africa and took the fight to Carcer. Sandra killed Alice Carcer, the head of the company, and we escaped with the new technology after Moss realized how powerful his program is.

"Turns out, the technology is going to be very helpful to us. Carcer is working with NeoVerge Industries to bring their military corporate rule to every planet and the tech we stole is a communicator. With Judy's help, we are going to use the communicator, hopefully, to reach out to the planets that aren't under NeoVerge rule and get help and supplies down here while taking the fight to Carcer out there.

"In a moment, Judy is going to tell us how to use the new device, which is certainly going to be difficult. The additional difficulty is that the program in our little friend's head is starting to break down in a way we don't understand. Patchwork is going to help figure it out, but it could cause some … headaches…" he got a proud little grin. "Long and short of it is, the big companies are evil and we are working to stop them, but we have a long way to go. Did I miss anything?"

Issy looked as if she was about to speak but Judy cut her off. "Yes, you missed quite a bit," they said grimly.

Gibbs flushed and nodded. "Right, sorry," he gulped. "We have lost a lot of good people along the way. We've been betrayed and people have died."

Judy nodded first and everyone else followed suit.

"Thank you all for letting me be a part of this," Issy said. "Together, we can end this fight and honor the fallen." She lifted a glass of wine and everyone did the same.

"To the fallen," Judy said, and everyone drank. Moss was impressed once again with the easy charm Issy possessed. She had done more to ingratiate herself in one minute than Moss felt he had done in his first month.

"Okay," Ynna said when the moment had passed. "Now that we have the previously-on out of the way, Jude, what are we looking at?"

Judy grabbed a metal box out of the corner and set it down on the table with a thud so powerful it rattled the glasses.

"Sure," they said. "I'll try to dumb this down for all of you since I don't think anyone here could parse the technical jargon." Moss smirked at the fact that Judy could often be insulting without meaning to. "This is basically just a connector piece which makes the communication array between here and a satellite network off-world work. I have no doubt that since we stole it, NeoVerge and Carcer have been working to replace it. In fact, with how long it took you guys to track me down, I expect that they already have."

Ynna sighed loudly to get attention. "Don't tell me that we did all this for nothing."

Judy chuckled. "No," they said. "Far from it. Having access to this has given me insight into how the whole system works, and with Patchwork's help, we are going to be able to hack their system and piggyback. We will be able to communicate with Anders's contacts."

"But?" Ynna asked.

"But we have to get close enough to replace the one they have put in with our own," Judy explained, their words making it clear how important this was.

"Ha," Gibbs said. "I mean, it's been like a day since we broke into something."

Everyone chuckled.

"Right," Judy said and smirked. "Well, at least this is an interplanetary company rather than a military one."

Gibbs snickered. "I guess that's something, anyway."

Issy raised her hand again to more amusement from the room and Moss smiled, knowing she was doing it for their benefit.

Judy looked at her. "Yes?"

"I understand that we want to warn the off-worlders that Carcer is coming for them, but if we are risking our necks, what is it that we are getting from them?" Issy asked.

Sandra snorted. "I like this one."

Anders, who tended to stay quiet at times like this, cleared his throat and all eyes turned to him.

"Supplies," he said. "If we have any hope of taking the fight to Carcer and ThutoCo and all the other members of the Amalgamated Interests Council, we need a lot more stuff than we can get down here. We have to arm an entire city at first and a planet before too long. We could never steal enough weapons from Carcer piecemeal. We need industrial production, and the off-world colonists can provide that. We can incentivize them by making it clear that as long as we are fighting Carcer here, they will have a harder time invading there. Additionally, we can offer them supplies in the future once we take over the world's food production from the likes of ThutoCo."

"Okay," Issy said.

"Think they'll go for it?" Gibbs asked dubiously, and Moss wondered if the doubt was more about Gibbs's lingering resentment than about anything actual.

"No reason they shouldn't," Anders observed. "That being said, the planets who are not under NeoVerge rule do not speak with a single voice. Everyone has their own interests, so there are those who may require more convincing. My friends will help."

"That just leaves the small matter of breaking into another, I'm assuming well-guarded, facility..." Ynna announced ominously.

"Yes, the communication tower is on the east side of the city," Judy said. "We will have to get this box to the top of the array, but it's surveilled by security drones around the clock."

"We could have Anders hover over," Gibbs began.

"Could save ourselves some trouble and just shoot our way in," Sandra said, and everyone began to offer ideas at once.

"Pardon," Puck said, quietly at first. "Excuse me," he said, a little more loudly. No one paid him any mind.

"Hey!" Moss yelled. "Everyone shut the fuck up a second."

The room fell silent, everyone seeming surprised by the sudden outburst. Moss gestured to Puck.

"Thank you for that charming introduction," Puck said and stood theatrically, sweeping his leg out from around his chair with flourish. "I know you all love to sally forth into the fray, but might there be a more clever option?"

He paused a moment for dramatic effect, waiting for someone to take the bait. Moss did, saying with exaggerated interest, "What did you have in mind?"

"Well, my lad, rather than attempting to penetrate the facility ourselves, might we try to turn someone who works there to our cause and have them do the job for us?" he said, steepling his fingers.

"Just buy someone off?" Ynna scoffed. "The companies all make it pretty clear what happens to employees who take candy from strangers."

"Why, certainly, but is it not possible to use young Patchwork to find someone with a skeleton in their closet who might be swayed?" Puck raised an eyebrow.

The room was quiet as everyone considered his words. "Why do the work ourselves when we can make some pedo do it for us?" Puck added.

"Not a bad idea, really," Sandra observed, scratching at her chin.

"The best solution is not always the most laborious one," Puck said.

Sandra held up her hands. "Yeah, you made your point. Hitch that high horse a moment and let's think on this."

"I'm happy to hack the employee database and start looking into those closets online," Patchwork said. "But I have to do one thing first."

All eyes returned to Moss.

"You know what you're looking for?" Moss asked. He was excited to finally have his friend look into the program, but it was more than a little scary to have someone hacking his own mind.

Patchwork looked at all the eyes around the table.

"Let's take this to my computer," he offered quietly, and Moss agreed.

"You guys keep coming up with ideas," Moss said to the room, and they all went back to thinking out loud — though it was clear they were still watching Moss and Patch.

They stood, Moss frowning at the uneaten food on his plate.

Issy caught his look. "I'll keep it warm for you," she offered, and reached out to squeeze his hand.

Moss took a deep breath and followed Patchwork into his room. An air mattress largely made up of duct tape sat on the floor with a blanket and long, human-sized pillow with an anime cartoon stitched on the front. A folding table had been set up for his computer supplies and projected screens. Cords and cables snaked everywhere. A few posters leaned against the wall to be hung later. The top one featured a half-naked woman covered in blood and standing over the bodies of corporate looking men. Moss recognized the movie and had even watched *Suit Slayer* with Gibbs a few years earlier.

His eyes narrowed as he stared at the sword in the young woman's hand. "No," he muttered, and Patch looked up, following his eyes.

"Oh, yeah," Patch said.

"All that for a fucking prop," Moss shook his head.

Patchwork stepped between him and the poster, drawing Moss's attention. "Look, it's not just any prop. Corp's Bane is a piece of film history. It was made in New Zealand and flown all the way to Japan for the movie."

Moss just shook his head.

"And anyway," Patchwork said, "it's not like I knew it was going to get me abducted by The Legion."

"Suppose that's true," Moss admitted. "Give me one sec."

He ran out, checking with Sandra before returning with the burlap wrapped item. Patchwork's eyes widened.

"Noooooo," he gasped. "No f-ing way!"

Moss unwrapped the prop, lifting the samurai sword by the handle before handing it over. Patchwork grabbed it like a kid grabs a cookie. He swung it around with precise movements, beaming and looking like he might cry with elation.

"Thanks, man!" he cheered.

Moss smiled, happy to bring some joy to the young man to whom he had brought so much misery.

After a while, Patchwork put down the blade and looked at Moss. "Okay, you ready to take a look at this program?"

"Yes," Moss said nervously. "I am."

CHAPTER 12

Patchwork had Moss lie down on the air mattress and turn to face the wall.

"Just going to have this reader close so it syncs faster," he told Moss. "Would love to hardwire it but I'd have to cut open your head."

"Rather you didn't," Moss said, trying to sound causal.

"Exactly," Patch said. "Here's the thing, I haven't done anything like this before, so you'll have to bear with me. We will learn together, but by the sound of it, there is a lot going on in your head. I'm going to do my best, but you have to know this shit is crazy, okay?"

Moss didn't like the sound of that though he knew it was true. This program had become as dangerous as it was powerful. For as little as he could control parts of it, being able to hack systems so easily was invaluable.

"I'll work with you, but you have to know . . ." he didn't want to finish the sentence.

"I know you are scared and you should be," Patchwork said. "But we'll figure this out."

The words didn't ease Moss's mind.

"Okay, I'm synced to your chip. Ready?" Patch asked, his eyes on his screens.

"Not really," Moss admitted.

"Should we do it anyway?" he asked.

Moss closed his eyes and tried to enter the program. It had been difficult so often, but within a moment he was back in the hex.

"Normally, you run the program through your computer in the hex?" Patchwork asked, his voice piped into the space from a speaker in the room.

"Yes," Moss said, standing from his bed. "Can you see me?"

Patchwork laughed, a computer-generated sound. "Sorta. I mean, it's all code to me."

"Of course."

"So," Patchwork said. "Tell me what you know for sure."

Moss had to think about that a moment. "I know my dad is in the program. He put himself in here using the technology he created. I know he shows up sometimes but not others, and that I cannot control it.

"I know that when I am in here, time does not pass in the outside world the same way because this seems to be more like thinking. But when I interact with the world, use the computer to hack or communicate, time flows normally."

"So far, that adds up," Patch agreed. "It's been about a minute in real-time since you have been interacting with me and I'm poking around. What else?"

"I know there is hacking software embedded in the program. It's been made super easy for me. All I have to do is use a drop-down menu and I can access it. What's strange is that I couldn't access it until I knew about it," he explained.

"That *is* interesting," Patchwork said. "The program is evolving and unlocking as you interact with the system. Those kinds of additions are difficult to write."

"How does it look on your end?" Moss asked, genuinely curious to know what the program was all about.

The synthesized laugh. "Don't have much for you yet. I want to know more. All I can tell you so far is that parts of this program are over a decade old, so there's a lot here I have to learn. Computer language evolves so I'm still finding my feet out here. What else can you tell me?"

"Recently, it has not just been my dad, but other people as well — people from my life and my past who should not exist in here," Moss admitted. This was where it was getting hard to understand.

"I see," Patchwork said, his voice a little uneasy.

"What?" Moss asked, stopping in his tracks. He only then realized he had been pacing around the space, walking back and forth between his little kitchen area and his desk.

"These neural chips are really common, but they are designed specifically to not do what you are describing," Patchwork told him.

"What am I describing?"

"This program is obviously generating code from your mind," he said bluntly.

Moss had suspected that had to be the case, but it worried him. "So my mind and the program are fusing?"

"Put plainly," Patch agreed. "Would your mom have had access to learning algorithms like that?"

"Yes," Moss said. "The whole point of the AI personalities of the drudges we work with is both based on us and adaptive. ThutoCo loves to say you "work with yourself," since the personalities are based on your own."

"There it is," Patch said. "Well, your mom used that to make this whole program adaptive in the same way. Problem is, since no one taught you how to use it, your brain and the program are just mingling."

"Awesome." Moss sighed in exasperation.

"It *is* awesome," Patch corrected. "Once we learn to harness this, you will be able to control this program and having it learn from you will only make things easier for you. Your parents gave you one of the most powerful gifts anyone has ever had. You just need to understand it."

"I like the way you think," Moss said.

"Let's try something," Patchwork said, and Moss looked around expectantly. Nothing happened and Patchwork didn't say anything.

"Am I missing something?"

"Stand by," Patch said.

Moss waited another moment before turning at the words, "Hey, kiddo."

His father was standing in the hex now. He always appeared in the same khaki pants and a blue button-up shirt he had loved in life. Gray crept into the base of his brown hair and his eyes were bright.

"Hey, Dad," Moss said with a cautious smile.

"Holy shit, you should see this thing," Patch said, and Moss's father turned.

"What's that?" he asked.

Moss breathed out a labored laugh and just shook his head. "That's Jo's son. In here to sort out what's been going on with this program."

His dad smiled. "Hey there, Willis."

"Hiya, it's Patchwork now and don't mind me," Patch said, "but holy shit this program you created is amazing."

"My team, really, and it took years of research," and Moss could see his father's smile of pride. "How'd you make out with those bounty hunters? Guess you survived since we are here."

What had just been the day before felt like a lifetime ago. "Yeah, made friends with them."

"For a price!" Patch threw in. "It took me all day to sneak money from enough accounts to pay off all those freelancers."

"But now we have more allies."

"Sure. Was a pain in the ass is all I'm saying," Patchwork said.

"I thought we weren't supposed to mind you," Moss smirked. Nothing more from the speaker, so Moss turned back to his father. "Took your advice," he said.

"What's that?"

"Realized we didn't have to shoot our way out of the situation," Moss told him. "Used my brain instead. What's left of it, anyway."

"That's wonderful," his father said. "The sign of a real leader is an ability to learn, adapt and grow. To listen to those around and come up with the best solutions."

"I'm coming to see that," Moss said, thinking about Steampuck the moment before. "We have a good crew and a lot of good ideas these days. I think we are making good progress."

"Toward?"

Moss had to think about that. "Toward a future where people are free to be who they want to be, and not just cogs in a global industrial machine."

His father smiled broadly. "That's a good goal. It was what I want, or wanted, too. I had spent so much time as a corporate shill that I had become blind to what they were really doing there. When I first realized that ThutoCo thought of its employees as literally disposable, I had to do something. I couldn't be prouder that you are doing the same. Except…"

"Except?" Moss asked.

"I already told you, I hate the risk you are taking."

"Your mom is keeping me safe," Moss told him, a bit petulantly.

"Good."

"And," Moss began, not because it was entirely relevant but because he just wanted to share the information, "Issy showed up and we talked everything out."

Without missing a beat, Patchwork crowed, "Ooh," through the speaker like a live studio audience.

Moss closed his eyes and sighed before opening them to see a broad, amused smile on his father's face.

"Not you too," Moss groused, but he was happy.

"It's really good, son. This life is pointless without family. You don't want to save this world just for the people in it, but for the future. For your children, and theirs."

Moss threw his hands up. "Oh, come on, Dad. I said she was back, not that we were getting married or anything."

"You will," Patchwork added, delight clear in his words.

"Will you fuck off," Moss said.

"Nah, this is too much fun and I'm learning a lot," Patch said, and even through the program Moss could hear the shit-eating grin.

His dad stepped forward. "If it's her, tell her."

"When did this become an after-school special?" Moss complained, but he was happy to be getting fatherly advice, even if just from a program. "Thanks."

His father smiled sweetly. "What are digital dads for?"

"Seems like a natural stopping point," Patchwork said. "Moss, mind if I turn him off?"

"Bye, Dad," Moss said and embraced his father, who evaporated in his arms.

"This is a trip, man," Patchwork said.

"Imagine how I feel."

"Can't even," Patch chuckled. "Now that I understand how the program generated your father, I need to get how it's creating people from your mind. Who have you seen in here? I assume they are all versions of people the way you remember them?"

That's when it clicked for Moss. His mother had appeared as his memory of her. It was also why she couldn't recall anything which didn't come from his own mind. It should have been obvious to him, but hearing Patchwork's words lifted the fog.

"Yes, that's it. I've seen Issy, my mom and Stan."

"Oh," Patchwork said sadly. "I miss Stan."

Moss's heart broke again, as it did every time he thought of his friend.

"Me too," Moss said. Even with Patchwork right there in his mind, Moss felt alone. He walked over to his computer chair and sat down.

"Sorry," Patchwork said. "Can you think about the people you've seen here and I'll see if I can bring them out? This is where shit's gonna get real."

He didn't want to see a memory of Stan again and so he thought about his mother. It had soothed him to see her face, so he closed his eyes and tried to bring her to the forefront.

"Hi, Moss," he heard, and he was shaking his head before he even opened his eyes.

"Really?" Moss asked as he looked up to see the Butler twins, once again naked in their perfect forms.

"Hey man, don't blame me," Patchwork said. "Your mind wrote this code. Plus, this is way funner, I just wish I could see it rather than read it."

Moss disgusted himself as he stared at their flawless naked bodies. He averted his eyes. "Is there a point to this?"

"Try to make them do something with your mind," Patch suggested.

"You realize you are basically reading porn in another man's mind, don't you?"

"I never said *what* to make them do, just try to control the program with your mind," Patch said. "You are creating them, remember? You can control them."

"I don't know how," Moss said. He felt miserable and weak.

"You do," Patchwork reassured him. "You can go into and out of the program. You can generate these people from your own memory. It's remarkable. If you can do all of that, you can change their code."

Moss opened his eyes and focused. Nothing happened at first, but as he worked at it, he felt something happen and clothes appeared on both of the girls.

"You are just straight up no fun," Patch complained.

Moss didn't care. He was just pleased that he was able to control the program. He always felt as though he was playing catch-up and now, perhaps, he could get out in front of it. He punched the air in joy.

"Yeah, man," Patch said. "You did it."

He harnessed the feeling of accomplishment into more thoughts and willed the girls away. He thought about Gibbs, who appeared for a moment, looked down at himself in confusion and said, "Weird," before vanishing too.

"This is amazing!" Moss said. As happy as he had been to see Issy, he was equally happy to feel that he had some mind control over the program.

He willed Patchwork into the hex and when he spoke now, the voice came from him. "All right, okay, give me a sec with all this."

"Sure," Moss said. He tried to picture the room from The Conservation and bring them there, but it didn't work. "How much will I be able to create?"

"Once you get a hold of this, you'll be able to create whatever you imagine. Just remember that it *is* just your imagination. You won't be able to learn anything from the things in the program."

"Could we change that? If the chip is connected to the internet, couldn't I also draw in knowledge from the outside world?" he asked excitedly.

"You know what," Patchwork said thoughtfully, "you are actually right."

Moss tried once more to move them to another place.

"Hold up," Patchwork said, raising his hands.

"What?" Moss said, still smiling.

"Oh, shit," Patchwork said, and Moss could feel his heart begin to pound and his palms sweat.

"What?" he asked again, but when he blinked he was alone in pure darkness. "Patchwork!" he cried. He didn't know where he was or what was happening. He looked around frantically for a way out. He tried to will his mind to return him to his hex.

Nothing.

"Fuck!" he screamed into the blackness. Had he broken the program? Was he now a prisoner of his own mind? Had his body died?

He fell to the ground in a ball, wrapping his hands around his knees.

Then he heard a vague crackling sound, small and distant. He squinted into the darkness and saw a dim orange flicker. He didn't know what it was, nor did he care. He stood and ran toward it. Slowly, it grew larger and the sound of fire came into focus. The orange began to stretch in both directions.

He could feel the heat on his body as he drew closer. A tall sheet of flames ran in both directions away from him. There was no smoke, just fire in the dark.

"Quite a literal interpretation," Patchwork said, and Moss turned to see his friend beside him.

"What is this?" Moss asked. "I mean, I know what it is, but why am I here?"

"We have problems," Patch said grimly.

"Yeah, no shit," Moss agreed. "People are trying to hack me?"

Patchwork nodded. "Yes. Seems like when I tried to look at the breakers, it pulled you here."

"What are they after? Can you tell who it is?"

"No idea and not yet," Patchwork said. "But I would assume they are trying to ping your location."

"Yeah."

"Not sure yet, but it seems like all the activity got their attention," Patchwork said.

"How is that possible?" Moss asked.

"Genuinely don't know, but you're lucky your mom was such a badass. Friggin' ten-year-old firewall still standing up to modern breakers. Impressive." Patch smiled, obviously in awe. "But if they are working round the clock on your head, we have problems."

"You mentioned," Moss said. The idea that people were trying to hack his mind all the time was a terrifying prospect. "What could they do if they got in?"

Patchwork's face fell. "That's the big question. I mean, you let me in and I was not able to control that much. But with time, I would have been able to really alter the code. If I could bring your dad to your hex, who knows what Carcer or ThutoCo could do if they got in."

"We can agree it would be bad.".

"Understatement of all time." Patch tried to joke but the words were dark. "Look, I'll get to work bolstering the firewall, but as soon as we are out, I have to get to work tracking down who's trying to crowbar your brain and you should probably give them a visit."

"You have a lot of work to do," Moss said, letting the moment hang before saying, "you know, we met your friend Zip."

Patchwork got a clever look, turned to Moss and gestured toward himself with hands in a 'come on' sort of move. Moss rolled his eyes.

"Zip Thud," he said.

Patchwork beamed. "It's really a good name," he laughed. "That kid's had a tough go. He acts like a badass, but he's a wounded child."

"Aren't we all."

Patchwork got a crooked smile. "Truer words…"

"Want us to bring him in? Think we can trust him?" Moss asked.

"Trust him, yes. Bring him in, not sure," Patch said. "Look, I need the help. As we get bigger we are going to need more bodies, but he may rub people the wrong way. Not that I know him that well, and he could surprise us, but he's an internet child — a screen orphan who won't know how to interact with real people. The way Ynna dresses, pretty sure Zip'll see as an opportunity to grab a piece."

Moss couldn't help but laugh at the image of that kid he had met on the street trying to get fresh with Ynna. "She'll break his hand in six places."

"Exactly. Breaker with a broken hand is like a dancer with a broken foot. Unless he has a neural link, but I doubt it. I think that kid spends too much on hookers."

"Not sure that detail was entirely relevant," Moss said.

Patchwork grinned. "Trying to paint you a picture."

"I got it," Moss said, slightly irritated. "I was just offering help. If you don't think he's a good fit, that's fine."

Patchwork held up his hands defensively. "That's not it. I think we probably should. I *do* need the help; I just wanted you to understand what you're getting into. Maybe warn Issy to guard her ass around him."

"The fuck is wrong with these kids?"

Patchwork laughed. "Like I said, raised by the internet. A kid who watched videos of facials all day isn't going to understand how real people operate."

Moss shook his head in disgust, his heart breaking for a generation. "All right; when we bring him in, I'll chat with him."

"Great," Patchwork said with a sigh that made it clear he had undersold how badly he needed help.

"Think we could carve out a little time every few days to do this again?" Moss asked. "I need to keep practicing in here and I seem to do better when I know you've got an eye on the code."

"Sure thing," Patchwork said. "But for now, let's check in with everyone. We have work to do."

CHAPTER 13

Moss stepped out of the car, feeling uneasy. His mind was swimming. He had been happy to take control of the program a little. Even though Patchwork hadn't provided any earth-shattering revelations, looking behind the curtain had helped. The equal and opposite part of learning that hackers were trying to pry open his mind worried him now every moment.

"You really didn't have to come," Moss told Ynna as she joined him on the street. She was the only one who had offered to come with him when Moss said he was going and while he was happy for the company, he was a little dubious as well.

"And miss an opportunity to teach some pervo a lesson? Not a chance," she said.

She had worn an outfit designed to 'mess with' Zip Thud, but before they had left, Moss saw Gibbs grimace as Ynna emerged from their room. Knee-high white socks, a Leia-style skirt which amounted to a strip of cloth along her front and back, her trademark leather jacket with a strip of cloth the width of a belt as a top and her pink hair pulled into pigtails. She looked like every nerd's wet dream.

A bright billboard overhead advertised cheap pets that barked and pawed from the display below. Tattoos were projected onto Moss and Ynna's faces as they passed a parlor, hearing the buzz from within. People crammed inside a restaurant and outside at a crowded adjoining parklet, drinking sake, smoking and popping sushi rolls in their mouths.

The two pressed themselves into the mob as a Carcer drone whirred overhead. They were much more common downtown. Here, the skies were a constant sea of activity. Delivery and security drones whirred around one another ceaselessly.

They kept moving once the drone had buzzed off.

The streets at night were always more active than during the day. The wide-open frontage of an arcade flashed like a dance club and young people moved from game to game, watching and one-upping one another.

"Kinda wish we could just stop in and play a while," Ynna said wistfully.

"Seriously, even ThutoCo used to let me take breaks once in a while."

"Don't let Sandra hear you talk like that," Ynna said, shooting him a smirk. "Y'all best be keeping them noses to the grindstone," she added in a mock impression of his grandmother.

Moss couldn't help but guffaw, snorting as he sucked in air. "Don't be doing nothern' weren't worth doing," Moss tried his best do recreate his grandmother's voice but it didn't work at all.

Ynna shrieked with laughter, punching him on the shoulder. "That one didn't even make sense."

"I know, I know," Moss said, still laughing. The two of them worked so tirelessly and so hard, they both needed a bit of fun.

As they passed a space between two buildings converted from an alleyway into a shallow ice cream shop, they shared a look. Neither spoke but both turned in unison.

"Two scoops of cookies 'n cream with marshmallow, caramel sauce and hot fudge in a waffle cone," Ynna said to the little robot in triangular paper hat. It plucked a cup in its two-pronged right hand and scooped with the spoon-shaped left.

"Order?" it asked of Moss, though the robotic voice made it sound more like a command.

"Cup with single scoop of vanilla with whipped cream and rainbow sprinkles," Moss said, checking once again to ensure the drones overhead were not Carcer.

Ynna was staring at him with an exaggerated look of amusement. "Of. Fucking. Course."

Moss breathed out slowly through his nose. People had loved to make fun of his simple taste for his whole life. Stan had worked hard to broaden his horizons, but he was still a vanilla kind of guy at heart. "I like what I like, so what?"

"Oh, nothing," Ynna shrugged but her face said it all.

"Hey, I'm doing pretty well given how I grew up," he said in justification as Ynna took her ice cream and transferred the money.

"You are," she said, dipping her spoon into her treat, a look of pure delight on her face. "I mean that sincerely."

"Thanks," he said, grabbing his ice cream. As he scooped in his first mouthful, the taste brought him back to a day in the burbs. It was one of the last days he had with his parents, one of the last times they were all together.

Moss had disappointed them, though they hadn't said it. His mother had helped him prepare late into the night but when he had done the presentation in class that day, he had forgotten what he had studied, flubbed his words and generally failed. The teachers' grade had been abysmal and he had done so poorly that even Gibbs didn't mock him.

He had sulked with his parents when he got home, curling up into his mother's arms. She had soothed him, but he could tell she was disappointed. She was naturally good at things and seemed confused when Moss didn't succeed. She was also a good parent and didn't scold him when he tried and failed, but there was always this little look she got that told him she was frustrated.

That look, more than just about anything else, had motivated him to do better. After his parents were gone, so too was the motivation. He would get the occasional spark when something inspired him, but he had mostly coasted once he was alone.

When his father had walked in to see Moss looking dejected, he suggested that the three of them go for a walk. Despite his disinterest in the idea, he had acquiesced and the three left their hex for the nearest food court two floors down. ThutoCo provided nicer food options than the ones served in the hex, but at cost and in designated eating areas. It was another way they incentivized their employees to leave their homes. Moss wouldn't find out until much later in life that it was a constant struggle for the company to keep their employees from gorging themselves and dying in solitude.

"You think ice cream would cheer you up, Mossy?" his father had asked.

"Doubt it," Moss replied. The open court was bustling and nearly every table was occupied. Each stall offered a different option from around the world. At the time, he had thought all the foods were gross or too adventurous for him, but when he finally left the burbs, he realized that even these international flavors were tepid versions of their real counterparts.

"Let's get some anyway," his father suggested with a smile.

"He said he didn't want any," his mom said.

Moss shook his head, not wanting them to fight. They rarely did, but there had been a tension in the house recently.

"Let's get some," he said, and they joined the short line. They wore their standard issue linens like everyone else there. The uniformity of his old life seemed so distant to him now.

"What happened?" his dad asked.

Moss dropped his head. "I don't know."

"He doesn't need to talk about it," his mother said in his defense.

"Thanks, mom," Moss said. "But maybe it's better if I do. I don't know what happened. I studied the material, I had my presentation ready, but when I got up in front of everyone it was like the knowledge just fell from my head."

"Stage fright?" his dad asked.

"No, not really," Moss said, trying to figure out what exactly he had felt in that moment. "I don't mind talking in front of people but, I don't know, something happened. It was like my brain was getting in its own way."

His parents shared a look. His dad put a hand on Moss's head. He usually hated that, but it didn't bother him then. "It's okay, Moss, it's totally natural," he told his son.

Moss's mom added, "You have good instincts, bubba bear, and a quick and agile mind, but you sometimes overthink things. If you would just act, you might be successful."

Moss furrowed his brows. "Shouldn't I be thinking? You guys are both thinkers."

"Yes," his father agreed. "We are, but we are also doers. Sometimes you have to be. Never forget that."

Moss never did. Even once they were gone and the general malaise set in on his life, Moss would sometimes just do as a way of honoring them. When he left the burbs for the city, he would sometimes just act. He would allow his instincts to guide him. As his parents had predicted, it usually worked.

They had not given him much more advice after that. They made small talk about some of the other kids' parents, work and *Burbz Haz Skills*, but Moss noticed something when they left the ice cream stall: his parents were holding hands. He had not seen much intimacy between them recently and it made him happy to know that something about the moment had brought them closer together.

"Thank you, come again," the robot said before demanding the order of the next customer. A line had formed in the time they had waited.

"You ever had ice cream with real milk?" Moss asked Ynna.

She nodded. "Rich kid," she reminded him through a mouthful. "You?"

"Yeah," Moss said. "Stan took me to an underground parlor in the Mission. I swear it was one of the best things I ever tasted."

They kept walking and Ynna said quietly, "Food was one of those things I didn't understand until I lost everything. In my young life, I just assumed everyone ate eight course dinners every night. It was a rude awakening when I had to start eating cereal for dinner every night because there was no one to cook for me and I didn't know how."

"I sometimes forget that you went through as jarring a transition as I did," Moss said. "You've been a badass as long as I've known you and I guess it's hard to picture you as some little princess."

Ynna chuckled. "If it's any consolation, it's *not* hard to picture you as a fucking bub."

"Yeah, yeah, yeah," Moss said. "Also, I've been meaning to thank you."

"Aren't you sweet," Ynna said. "And I certainly deserve it, but for what in particular?"

"Everything," Moss said. "It doesn't go unnoticed how much you do. Between missions, you are keeping everything together, updating Seti, caring for that little dog *and* Perro," he said with a wink and she giggled. "You hold this whole operation together and I want you to know I appreciate it."

"Thanks," she said quietly. "It can be a little frustrating. You grandmother is so exacting, and you are the fucking golden boy, but I'm still the one doing all the day-to-day work while also being expected to shoot our way out of messes.

"Don't get me wrong, after a childhood of being an ornament, I'm thrilled to be as valuable as I obviously am. It just gets to be a little much sometimes."

"I can appreciate that," Moss said. "You know that I'm happy to help in whatever way I can."

"I know, but you've got bigger fish to fry," she said. "As this thing gets bigger, you are going to have to be a leader out in front and I'm going to have to be behind the scenes. We both know that's the opposite of how it should be, but also that it is how it is."

"Right," Moss said.

"Anyway, I've got Gibbs to do my bidding," Ynna said with a laugh before dropping her cone wrapper on the ground before the wind carried it down the street to join a pile of garbage. She got a sassy look. "You must be happy Issy's back."

"Feels like high school with how often I'm having this conversation," he said.

"No, it feels like high school because we all know you like-like her," Ynna said, skipping around him.

He dropped his head in defeat. "Yeah, I do. I think we will make it work; it'll just take some time."

She stopped in front of him and looked right into his eyes with a genuine smile on her lips. "I'm really happy for you guys."

"I'm happy for you guys too," Moss said.

"Oh, don't get me started," Ynna rolled her eyes. "I'll never get why I like him, but I do."

He had never heard her admit it outright. "We're all growing up," Moss chuckled, thinking about the ring Gibbs had shown him.

Ynna put on an English accent, "Oh, why yes, Peter," she said and then covered her mouth in horror. "I really *am* becoming like him."

"It's cute," Moss said, trying to get her goat.

"You realize I can still kick your ass, right?"

Moss pointed down an alleyway. "I think it's just up here."

"Great," Ynna said with a grin. "Let's go set this kid straight."

Moss stopped and shook his head. "No, we are here to recruit him, remember?"

"Right," Ynna said as they started walking. "*And* set him straight."

Moss rubbed his face in exhaustion as they neared the end of a dark alley piled with bags of garbage. "Right. And set him straight."

Steepling her fingers, she announced, "Excellent."

Moss couldn't help but smile at the effect Gibbs was having on her. "Just keep in mind," Moss said, "Zip is a kid. A damaged kid who could use some mentors."

"Oh, I'll go all sorts of mentor on his ass," Ynna said, smirking.

"And we need his help," Moss reminded her.

"Okay, okay, okay," Ynna said, starting to seem genuinely annoyed. "I'll play nice," and after a quick beat added, "nice-ish."

Moss found the dumpster Patchwork had told them about. 8-bit eyes were spray-painted almost invisibly on a drainpipe nearby. Together, they slid the dumpster to one side, revealing a gap in the brick wall just large enough to crawl though.

"Ladies first," Ynna said, making a sweeping hand gesture toward the hole.

"Thanks," Moss said with an eyeroll and knelt to crawl into darkness.

CHAPTER 14

Moss felt his way forward, wishing once again for cybernetic eyes. They had digital contact lenses, lenscreens, at the safehouse but Moss almost never remembered to grab them before heading out. He heard muffled noise but couldn't tell quite where it came from. He kept moving forward, chunks of brick and dirt crunching into the palms of his hands.

Before too long, he reached the end of the tunnel, feeling a sheet of corrugated tin. It didn't take much to push it out of place and he was greeted by the dim glow of a room illuminated by computer monitors, both physical and projected. Moss squeezed through the hole at the other end to the overwhelming scent of nag champa. He gagged and coughed as he laboriously rose to his feet.

Cackling laughter filled the space as Moss looked up to see Zip Thud filming his inelegant movements. The kid was dressed in layered tight gray jeans, a translucent black shirt with three-quarter sleeves, fingerless gloves and a thick gray wrap draped over his head, neck and shoulders.

"Man, I could be rich with this shit," he shrieked in delight.

Moss groaned.

"One of the most wanted people on the planet crawling out of a hole," Zip laughed. "All to see little old me. Priceless."

He may have had the hacking abilities of a much older person, but he really was still a kid. Moss dusted the dirt and detritus from his hands, continuing to gag as his lungs filled with incense that was clearly being burned to mask the scent of body odor and gas.

The room was more spacious than Moss had guessed it would be. It was circular with doorless frames leading to three other spaces. Weathered wooden beads on string hung in each frame. A bright sign for Life Rider Beer acted as proper lighting for the space; the broad grin of a bearded and shirtless man holding forward two frosty brews stared down at Moss. There were screens everywhere and it took Moss a moment to notice there was another young person laying on a beach towel on the exposed cinderblock floor. She was jacked directly into the computer networks.

The room was a jungle of cords and cables. Zip's eye plates were not active and all Moss saw was his own tired reflection looking back at him.

"So, what brings you crawling back to me?" the kid asked with a self-satisfied smirk.

Moss sighed.

Zip cocked his head. "See what I did there?"

"Yes," Moss said in the same patronizing tone he used with Gibbs when he explained a joke.

A cough came from the hole as Ynna clambered out. She looked up at Zip with disgust.

"What's this?" he asked, his eyes scanning her as she got to her feet, flicking at the brown stains on her white socks.

"Ynna," Moss said. "Another member of the team."

Zip turned his eyes on so he could roll them. "Well, if she's here as a gift of whatever, no dice. I'm RBS and proud."

Moss turned a quizzical look to Ynna. "Robosexual," she said.

"Yeah," Zip said. "I like my parts to be parts, know what I mean?"

Moss did. He had known quite a few people in the burbs who preferred relief aides to other humans. Robots did what they were told when they were told, and some folks found that easier than trying to cope with a partner. Moss's friend Ricky had explained that people were complicated and confusing and he simply found intimacy easier with a machine. Moss had come to understand that there was more nuance to it, but that explanation had sufficed at the time.

"So, I don't want any of this," he said, making a circular motion with a flat palm toward Ynna.

"It's not on offer," Ynna said. She had come in with a plan but crawling through a dark cave and the kid's honesty about his sexuality had obviously thrown her.

The 8-Bit eyes rolled again. "Tell that to your outfit."

Ynna moved forward threateningly. "How I dress shouldn't affect how you speak to me," she said through gritted teeth, her fists balled.

Zip held up his hands, backing up as the eyes went wide and curved brows appeared to indicate his fear. "Yeah, all right, sorry," he stammered, tripping over a coiled cord on the ground but catching himself. "Look, it's just that you showed up in what amounts to twenty-five square centimeters of clothing and it sometimes takes me a minute to speak to people normally, you know?"

Ynna's hand fell open. "Yeah, I know," she said.

"I really am sorry," he said. "I didn't mean any disrespect. It's just that you gotta be hard and gross online."

"No, you don't," Moss said and both Zip and Ynna looked at him pityingly.

"Kid's obviously playing a character," Ynna told Moss. "Don't think we have much to worry about."

"Nah, I'm good people. If I do say so myself. And I do."

Ynna laughed. "Well, we crawled into your rat's lair. You going to offer us something to drink?"

"Oh, um, yeah, sure," Zip said with a little smile and hustled into another room, the beads ticking against one another after he left.

Moss turned a grin on Ynna. "Your attitude changed quickly."

"Yeah," she shrugged. "I could tell in a sec that Patch read him wrong. And anyway, he kind of reminds me of myself. I wasn't much older than he is when I had to start fending for myself. You know, he's the type we are doing all this for."

"Sure," Moss agreed.

"Now I just kinda feel like an asshole in this getup," she admitted.

Moss chuckled. "It was a weird plan anyway," he smirked.

"Oh, fuck off. All of my plans are gold," she said, playfully punching him on the shoulder with her cybernetic hand. He knew it would leave a bruise.

Zip returned with souvenir plastic cups from a chain restaurant, lighted from the base so the drinks glowed neon green. "Vodka and ZoomZoom," he said, holding the drinks out.

As he took it, Moss swirled it in the cup. The drink was pungent enough to cut through even the incense. He grimaced and Zip noticed. "It's all I got."

"No, it's fine, thanks," he said, taking a sip that tasted like paint thinner with aspartame.

"Patch said you have an offer for me," Zip said. "What's up?"

"We want you to come work with us," Moss said. "Help the little guy, as you put it."

"Cool, cool, cool," Zip said. "Why?"

"Because we need your help," Ynna said as she finished the drink and set it down on a desk constructed of nailed together wooden pallets.

"No, I got that part," Zip said. "I meant, what's in it for me."

"It's the right thing to do," Moss said, but the words sounded lame even to him.

Zip Thud frowned. "That's your best pitch?"

"What do you want?" Ynna asked in annoyance.

Zip smiled and rubbed his hands together. "Now you're speaking my language."

"Everyone speaks this fucking language these days." Ynna sighed and turned to Moss. "Maybe we are the dumb ones; we do all this shit for free."

"Oh, we are definitely the dumb ones," Moss agreed with a laugh.

Zip asked, "You guys an item?"

The two looked at each other, laughing and shaking their heads. "She's really not my type," Moss said.

"Right back atcha, slick," Ynna said mockingly.

"Okay," Zip said as though he didn't believe them.

Even though it was true, the moment was still awkward and Moss broke the silence. "What is it that you want?"

"An upgraded part for Belle," he said, pointing to the person on the ground. Moss realized then that she wasn't jacked in, but charging. The machine was thoroughly lifelike and Moss was surprised that the kid could have afforded one. Unlike the relief aides who were sent to his hex, the android on ground was dressed modestly. She wore a simple pink hoodie with a couple of the D2E princesses on the front and Comph brand sweatpants with the company name emblazoned on the right leg. The pants were a bit of a surprise to Moss. They were famously soft and therefore notoriously expensive and not something a person would necessarily buy their machine.

"Can't you just buy them?" Moss asked. "We already have a lot of moving parts."

"You want my grease for those parts?" Zip asked sarcastically. "Then help me out."

"Fine." Moss sighed. "What do we need to do?"

"No big deal, really," Zip said while Moss and Ynna shared a dubious look. "I got outbid for a SOFThide Mk. II they don't make anymore. It was easy to hack the dick who won, so all we need to do is stop by his place and get the hands."

Ynna grimaced. "Don't judge," Zip said. "I'll wash them. I'm not trying to swap shaft juice here."

"We aren't thugs for hire," Moss said, feeling like he had to make that argument a lot.

Ynna scoffed. "Sure we are."

"No," Moss said, a little annoyed now. "All the guy did was outbid you; there is nothing inherently wrong with that. I'm not going to go intimidate him for you."

"That's cool, I get it, but also . . ." he trailed off, turning his back on them and moving toward his black gaming chair with yellow trim.

"The fuck difference does it make?" Ynna asked.

Moss narrowed his eyes at her. "It's an innocent guy."

"Would it help if I told you he works as a Carcer recruiter, convincing good people to work for an evil company?" Zip asked.

Ynna beamed. "There you go," she said, patting Moss on the cheek.

"We good?" Zip asked.

Moss sighed. "Fine."

Zip got up from his chair and knelt by Belle, unplugging her and clicking her ear back into place to hide the charge port. He whispered some command and she sat up, stretching naturally.

Moss marveled that if he didn't know she was a machine, he probably would not have been able to figure it out.

"Greetings," she said a little stiffly. "I am Belle. It is a pleasure to make your acquaintance."

She held out a straight arm.

"Moss," he said, shaking her hand. He hooked a thumb. "Ynna."

"Good to meet you," Belle said. "Zip's friends are so good looking."

Ynna stifled a laugh. "Thanks," she said. "You're cute too."

"Thank you," Belle said. Her blond hair was pulled back into a large bun and held down with a powder blue headband. She had unnaturally large blue eyes, perfect pink lips, flawless skin and a little nose that people would go under the knife for. She wore large shimmering oval earrings and a little black choker around her neck.

"We are going to get you some new hands," Moss told her.

"What?" she said, tilting her head in confusion.

Zip shook his head violently from behind her. Moss understood. "Nothing," he amended.

"No," she said, "I want to know what you meant by that."

Moss had hoped she would drop it and didn't really know what to say in this situation. He opened his mouth but Ynna saved him. "I really love your top," she said.

"Aw, thanks," Belle said. "I got it when he took me to D2Eland."

"That's sweet," Ynna said, and Belle took a step forward. The movement was fluid but so rapid that it took Moss by surprise.

"Who's your favorite princess?" she asked Ynna in a conspiratorial tone.

Moss wanted to laugh at the absurdity of asking a woman like Ynna something like that.

Ynna smiled almost bashfully. "I was always partial to Princess Renee."

Belle held her hands to her heart. "Oh, I love her too."

"We will send someone to have your stuff brough to our safehouse," Ynna told Zip.

"Oh," he said in surprise. "We're moving in?"

"Easier that way," Moss said.

"Um, okay, I guess," Zip said, sounding unhappy about the situation.

"It'll be so fun," Ynna said to Belle, who squealed with delight.

"Well played," Zip said in defeat. "Guess things happen fast."

Moss laughed. "You have no idea."

The four reached the apartment complex minutes later. The building was divided into four layers, each with their own entrances and elevator systems. The first layer had the most floors and apartments, each one small and cheap. They became larger and more costly as they got closer to the top. The highest two layers were only accessible by landing a flighted car on a pad. Luckily, they were going to the second layer.

The elevator to reach the lobby was on the outside of the building and required a passcode that Zip Thud had easily acquired before they left. They rode the elevator up to nauseating heights. As Belle oohed and awed, Moss gripped the handlebar tightly. He was the first one out when they reached the lobby. It was a large space with two circular sitting areas set into the floor around false firepits. A few small shops lined the walls selling just enough goods that a person could do any necessary shopping even though a delivery drone door was installed next to the elevator.

It was quiet at this time of night and all the shops that didn't rely solely on computer kiosks were manned by drudges. As the four made their way through the lobby, they heard a quiet ding from behind before a drone carrying a pizza box flew through the designated drone delivery door and disappeared down a hallway.

"Know where we are going?" Moss asked.

Zip nodded and turned to face Belle and Ynna. "Why don't you guys wait here?"

Ynna's face contorted. "I'm better at … asking for things … than he is," she said.

Zip looked her over. "That may usually be true, but you aren't particularly intimidating at the moment," he said, sounding a little fearful.

Ynna groaned, looking at herself in the reflection of a glass storefront. "I'm fucking done discussing my outfit choices, like ever. I could still kick all of y'all's asses."

Moss nodded. "We know, we know."

He followed Zip down a hallway that seemed to stretch on forever. Door after nondescript door. The same patterned carpet. The same ads running in the same digital picture frames.

Eventually, Zip stopped and knocked on one of the doors. Moss was caught by surprise but stopped, turned and waited. A beam of yellow light showed under the door, easy to see in the dimly-lit hallway.

"Who is it?" a woman's voice asked through the door.

Moss looked at Zip, who was staring at him intently.

"Repairman," Moss said, trying to think of something on the fly. He had expected Zip to come up with a plan, but he had simply set it in motion.

"What are you here to fix?" the voice asked.

"Fire alarm, ma'am," Moss said, inadvertently putting on a false voice.

"Can't that wait until morning?"

"No, ma'am," Moss continued. "In order to comply with fire code, we must fix it immediately. Been going door to door but there are hundreds of apartments in this building. I do apologize for the hour."

"Oh, okay" the voice said, and they could make out her whispering to someone away from the door.

"Also, I don't think you could sleep soundly knowing you could be cooked alive in a fire," Moss added for good measure. Standing out of sight of the peephole camera, Zip gave a thumbs up.

A man's voice boomed. "This is highly irregular, I'm going to call the manager."

"I am the manager." Moss scrambled to think of something, but Zip was already getting to work. He unfolded a tablet and began tapping furiously.

"I'm here to help and I would be more than happy to show you my credentials if you open the door," Moss said, but even as he said the last part, he thought he may have overplayed his hand.

"I thought you said you were a repairman, and why can't you show me your creds through the door?" the male voice demanded. "This building is under Carcer Corporation protection. I think it's time we give them a call."

Moss swallowed hard, realizing the situation had just become much worse than he expected. He heard a beep and to everyone's surprise the door hissed open. The two naked people behind the door stared at Moss with wide eyes as he did the same. The woman was unnaturally curvaceous, with platinum hair, massive red lips and angular features. The man was muscular for his age and tanned in the way only a machine could create. His skin was pulled right over his bulging muscles and he was shaved from head to toe.

The instincts kicked in.

Before he even knew what was happening, the Kingfisher was out and sending blue flashes. The man shook and crumpled to the floor in a heap, but the woman froze in place when the bolt hit her and she collapsed backward with a solid thud.

Zip pushed Moss through the door and it closed quickly behind him. Moss stepped over to the man to make sure he was still breathing. He was and would be fine. Zip set to work. He flipped open the woman's ear and pressed the button next to the power source to open the panel at the base of her skull. Atsuko AndroiTech placed the controls where there tended to be hair, so it was more difficult to see. Some of the most advanced models didn't even have panels, relying exclusively on remote systems.

He selected a few options and Moss heard the click at the machine's wrists. Zip quickly pulled a special razor from his pocket, pulled off the cap and cut near the wrist where an indicator light shone through the skin.

There was no blood and the nanotech skin would reattach when applied to the next body. Zip beamed up at Moss who just rolled his eyes and looked at the nice apartment. It was spacious and had a gorgeous view of the surrounding buildings and layers of dotted traffic streaking through the sky.

As Zip pulled the first hand free, Moss's eye caught a photo hanging on the wall. The naked man on the floor was standing at a holiday party wearing a red and green knit sweater that read, "RePurp Industries."

Moss's eyes narrowed.

"I thought you said he was a Carcer recruiter," Moss seethed. He hated being played for a fool.

Zip looked up at him nervously as he sliced at the second hand. "No, I asked if it would help if that's what I said," he justified, his tiny body shrinking down and away from Moss whose hand was lifting the barrel toward the kid.

"Oh, come on, man," Zip said tremulously. "We've come this far."

Moss thought about it for a moment before he heard Ynna in his mind, *we gotta go!*

"Shit, it's time," Moss said and yanked the hand the rest of the way off, shoving it into Zip's chest and pressing the door's unlock button. They ran. Zip's legs were short, but he ran with the speed of youth, darting down the hall in a flash. Moss's robotic legs carried him, easily keeping pace.

As they rounded the final corner back into the lobby, they saw Belle cowering in the elevator with Ynna holding the door open. A crumpled security guard lay on the floor nearby.

Ynna waved them in, brandishing the guard's taser in one hand. "There'll be more."

Zip was visibly terrified and Belle was shaking with fear. As the door slid closed, Moss watched her hands tremble.

CHAPTER 15

They could see the Carcer vehicles making their way toward the building as the elevator dropped toward the ground.

"Damn," Ynna said, watching them close in.

"Think they'll get here before we can get away?" Moss asked, trying to calculate the distance.

"Hard to tell," she said, trying to do the same thing.

We need backup, Ynna communicated to the team back at the safehouse, but she and Moss knew there was no way the crew could reach them in time.

Copy that, Sandra's voice told them. It didn't matter. The elevator would be at the bottom of the tower before they could even get their shoes on.

"We're going to die, we're going to die," Belle was muttering in the corner of the elevator. Zip Thud's petrified body didn't move. Moss didn't even know if he was breathing. Like Patchwork, Zip's skills were behind a monitor. Unlike Patchwork, he seemed to have no combat training of any sort, no veteran mother who forced him to learn basic skills and no desire to teach himself the samurai sword.

"Zip," Moss said, and the kid's eyes snapped to him. In that moment, he looked like a child, his face miserable and scared.

Moss sympathized with the kid who had been forced to grow up too fast. Moss wanted to help him, to teach him the way so many had helped and taught him. "She's scared," he told the young man, who turned to look down at his love. He knelt as the elevator continued to drop and the flashing lights moving toward them continued to increase in numbers.

He watched as Zip tried to console Belle, but she yelled in a voice too amplified to be natural, "Do something!"

Moss smiled slightly as Zip pulled out his tablet once more, fumbling as he unfolded it; his hands were shaking so hard. His eyes darted between the Carcer cars and his tablet. He took a deep breath, calming his body and began to work. Moss watched as lights shone behind his eye plates. Text poured down the screen and Zip's fingers were working faster than he had ever seen anyone's fly.

"Crap," Zip complained to himself.

They were nearing the ground and the cars were only a few blocks away, but the security drones were already waiting for them. Looking through the glass of the elevator as they neared the bottom, Moss understood how fish must feel looking up at the barrel of the gun. He gripped his Kingfisher, setting it to lethal, but knew it was pointless. If they got into a fair fight, they would lose.

"Hacking Carcer is nearly impossible," Zip groused, his voice cracking. Kids his age should have been whining about their homework or parents, not trying to break into the world's largest private military.

"If it was easy," Moss said, "we wouldn't need *you.*"

Though Zip was almost too distracted to notice the words, Moss saw him smile.

"Right," he said, and Moss could feel the determination emanating from the young man. Ynna winked at Moss.

"I believe in you, sweetie," Belle said, drying her tears. Moss wondered for just a moment how much of her personality had been programmed by Zip himself. As the first Carcer van pulled into the circle at the base of the building, a single drone began to climb toward the elevator.

Moss knew that the moment Carcer identified who was riding in the elevator, they would be killed. So far, they had been lucky that this had seemed like a routine break-in, but that was about to change. Moss and Ynna flipped on the scramblers sewn into the collars of their jackets and covered their faces for good measure, but that would only last so long.

From between his fingers, he saw the camera of the circular drone topped with flashing light begin to focus. The gun hanging from the bottom didn't move as the scramblers did their job. An operator would take manual control any second.

Moss's fears were realized as a red light at the base of the weapon turned on.

Belle screamed.

Instinctively, Moss moved to cover her body with his. He sucked in a breath, waiting for the familiar feeling of being shot and the unfamiliar feeling of being killed.

"Yes!" he heard Zip cry and turned to watch the drone spin. The other drones were hovering like buzzards as the elevator stopped at the bottom.

Ding.

The elevator door opened as the drones opened fire.

The Carcer operatives who had been waiting absently for the elevator to arrive screamed in shock as bolts pierced the night. The vehicles sizzled and popped as they were struck, shaking and rattling. The targeting systems of the drones worked perfectly with the flying machines banking and gliding to get better shots.

As quickly as the action had started, it ended.

One final Carcer officer slid down the hood of his car and flopped onto the ground.

Heading to the dropship now, getting a fix on your location, Gibbs informed them.

Moss and Ynna laughed. *Belay that request*, she told him, shaking her head.

Belle sprang to her feet, jumping on Zip who dropped his tablet as she kissed him all over his face. He smiled and sighed so hard that Moss wondered how long he had been holding his breath.

"Great work, kid," Moss said, clapping him on the back. The drones circled overhead, waiting for more vehicles to approach.

Zip exhaled again as Belle continued to kiss him. "I'm too relieved to even be bothered by the use of 'kid' just there," he said with a smile.

Moss scooped up the tablet. "Sorry," he said, handing it over. "Great work."

"Alright, love fest, can we haul ass please," Ynna interrupted. "That was just round one."

They all ran, Belle squeaking with delight as Zip pulled her toward the van by her old hand.

As they got in, Ynna fired it up and pulled out, setting a route for the nearest hideout. They had a network of spots around the city where they could lay low in a car if they were being followed but had lost their pursuers.

The tires screeched against the pavement and Zip got to work hiding them, using the hacked drones as bait. Ynna drove toward the Miner's Stadium District. The million-seat venue was a city unto itself, with tall apartment complexes that surrounded parts of the field and its own transit network. In the reflected light of the massive complex, Ynna pulled the van through a cut cloth that was painted to look like a wall. There were a few squat buildings next to them and the freeway ran above. A tarp pulled into a lean-to sat beside a concrete pillar thicker than the van.

Moss chuckled and reminded himself to tell Puck about the simplicity of this ruse.

"We good?" Ynna asked Zip.

He nodded. "I got the drones attacking the vans. They'll have no idea what hit them."

"Taste of their own medicine," Ynna said with a smirk.

"Oh, Zippy," Belle declared, "you were so brave! You saved our lives. Thank you. Thank you. Thank you." She wrapped her arms around him and held on.

"Seriously," Moss agreed. "You did good."

"Exhilarating, right?" Ynna asked.

Zip Thud's mouth formed a perfect circle. "Exhilarating?" he asked finally. "Terrifying."

Ynna laughed. "Sure, that too."

"Worth it?" Moss asked, extending a finger to poke at one of the hands in Zip's pocket. As the young man turned to speak, Moss amended, "On second thought, I don't want to know."

"You holding up okay?" Moss asked Belle, not because he particularly cared about the machine's opinion but because he knew it was important to Zip.

She looked down at her quivering hand. "I guess. I have never really seen anything like that before. I cover my eyes in the scary parts of movies. Why were those people going to shoot at us?"

"Because they are bad people," Moss said flatly, remembering the moment in the apartment just before all this began. He turned to Zip. "Also, you are lucky that you just saved my life."

"You care about that shit now?" Zip said in genuine astonishment. "We almost just died. Who cares that I tricked you?"

"I do."

"And we've *always* almost just died," Ynna added. Moss chuckled.

Belle looked at the two of them in disbelief. "Who are you people?"

Ynna winked at Moss and said dramatically, "We are the good guys."

They all took a moment to calm down, Ynna sharing sips from the car bottle. When she produced a pack of Longporks, Belle reached out for one. Moss couldn't hide his laugh, wondering how much the cigarette companies had paid the robotics makers for that.

"So," Zip said finally. "You did my thing, now what do you need from me?"

"We need you to infiltrate a Carcer prison," Ynna said deadly seriously, holding the taser out to him.

His digital eyes went wide once more. "What?" he murmured and Ynna couldn't hold it together any longer.

She burst out laughing and it wasn't long before Moss, and even Belle, were laughing too. "Sorry," Ynna said, "I just had to fuck with you."

"That was not very nice," Belle said, screwing up her face into a pout.

Zip snorted. "I heard you laugh."

"Sorry baby," she said with a guilty look. The expressions were unbelievably lifelike and a marvel of engineering, although these more affordable models looked strange when transitioning between expressions.

Moss remembered how real the androids he had met in Africa had looked, how convincing they were. It made him shudder to think back.

"I love you," Belle told Zip, putting a hand on his cheek and looking into his eye plates.

He smiled sweetly. "I love you too."

Moss and Ynna shared a look as the other two embraced and seemed as if they might begin to do more. Belle's hand moved down the kid's spine but stopped and she pulled away.

"What is this?" she accused as she pulled a Beretta from his belt.

Moss's eyes went wide with surprise and amusement. This kid, who had no business being in a fight in the first place, was carrying a loaded weapon.

"I just," Zip stammered. "I just carry it for protection sometimes."

"You know how I feel about guns!" she said, shoving it against his chest and causing everyone in the vehicle to recoil even though the safety was on.

"I know," he said. "I'm sorry, baby."

"Oh, do not, 'I am sorry, baby,' me!" Her face was red with anger and her eyes narrowed at Zip. Moss couldn't help but wonder what his friend Ricky would say about this fight and if there was some setting you had to turn on to have the machines behave this way.

Zip put the weapon back in his belt.

"You know that we are much more likely to be harmed with that in the house!" she continued and Moss just leaned back, taking in the moment.

"Yes," Zip said meekly. "It's a scary world out there."

"I think you know where you can stick those platitudes," Belle snarled.

"Hey, Belle," Ynna interjected, and Zip looked like he could have kissed her. "Want to go out for a smoke?"

"Yes, Ynna. Yes, I do."

The two stepped from the car, Belle slamming the door shut in a show of anger.

Once they were alone, Zip sighed. "Women, right?"

Moss rubbed his face with his hands. "Sure, let's go with that."

It was quiet in the back for a moment. The two sat on opposite sides of the van. There were little benches on either side and straps soldered to the wall to hold on to during a chase. There was a footlocker full of supplies they could have used a moment earlier if they had thought about it. A dome light in the middle provided just enough illumination for them to see one another.

"How old are you?" Moss asked.

"You going to make fun of my age? Lecture me or some shit?" Zip asked, his hackles up.

"No," Moss smiled. "I was asking because I'm impressed by you. You held your own with my grandmother when we first met, you negotiated me into doing a job, shut down Ynna and got us out of a scrape. It would be impressive for anyone. But for a person of, fourteen? Fifteen? It's remarkable."

Zip Thud smiled. "Fifteen," he said. "And thanks."

Moss shook his head, laughing. "Man, when I was fifteen, I couldn't have done everything you did today in a video game, let alone in real life."

"Oh," Zip said, seeming to have a moment of clarity. "You're a bub?"

"Yeah," Moss said.

"Well, if there is an opposite of growing up in the burbs, it's my life," Zip told him. "I think that poverty is the only trait my parents got from theirs. We moved to B.A. City when I was born because my family thought they would find a different life out here. Turns out we found the same life — just with fog instead of sand.

"And we were even worse off because my parents had spent what little they had just to get us here. We bounced from hovel to hovel, each one getting smaller and shittier until it was just the pavement."

"I'm sorry," Moss said. "I honestly didn't realize how good I had it in many ways growing up … I mean, good until the company my parents worked for killed them."

"Ah." Zip nodded before tilting his head to crack his neck. "Loan Collection Officers for mine."

"Tale as old as time."

"That's why you do this, right?" Zip asked, his voice sounding a little hopeful.

"It is," Moss said. "Kids shouldn't grow up without parents just because some company doesn't think their lives have value."

"I like it," Zip said. "I mean, I'll still want some form of payment, but I'm happy to be here helping."

"I'm happy we met, too," Moss said. "And Belle. She's sweet."

"Yeah," Zip agreed as he cupped his hand toward his eye plate and exhaled a little warm air before wiping the condensation with his sleeve. "She's a bit of a ball buster, but I like a challenge."

Moss didn't want to overstep but asked, "But you made her that way?"

Zip laughed. "I got her a year ago, used. She'd been wiped but still had a few personality mods. I changed a bit of her code in the beginning but left it alone ever since. I like that she doesn't always make things easy for me."

"Huh," Moss said, thinking about it. "The girl, I mean, well, the girl I want to date, am sorta dating … well, this girl … anyway … she challenges me too. Always has."

Zip gave a crooked smile. "They make us better."

"Yes, they do."

"You miss your parents?" The question was asked so quietly that it seemed a slight breeze could have carried it away.

Moss felt a choking emotion creep through him. His lips tightened as they strained against the feelings. "Every day," he admitted.

Moss could read the same experience on Zip. He was still struggling with the loss. Would always struggle with the loss. "Me too," Zip peeped.

Moss scooted from the bench and down on his knees across the van's hard metal floor van to put a hand on the young man's back. Being that close, Moss noticed how truly small he was. Moss was not large but even kneeling he seemed to tower over the kid.

"So what can I do?" Zip sniffled.

"Patchwork is busy looking into a way we actually can infiltrate a facility. What we need is for you to try and find the breakers who are trying to hack the chip in my mind."

Zip looked confused. "That's a standard ThutoCo neural comm chip?" he asked. "There isn't much to that and there is really nothing to be gained by getting into it."

Moss didn't even know what to say to that, there was just so much. "Well," he began. "My chip has a bit of extra data that a couple of the megas would be interested in."

"Megas?" Zip repeated. "What are you, from Europe? Don't really hear that too much stateside."

Moss laughed at himself. "Friend of mine says it and I guess it stuck. Matter of fact, I think the term is really making its way through the group."

"Heard," Zip said expectantly. The phrase was familiar, but Moss couldn't quite place it. "Patchwork says that, so now I do too," Zip explained.

"Ah."

"He must have worked in a restaurant or something."

"His mom's bar, but they do serve food," Moss said. "Well, food may be a generous term."

Zip laughed. "He's a good guy? Patchwork, I mean."

Moss nodded. It was odd to him that this friend of Patch had never actually met him. "He's one of the best. Said you were too. Even implied that you would be better at finding the breaker than he would be."

"Whoa." Zip beamed, taking in the praise for just a moment. "You want me to take a look?"

"Yes, please," Moss said. "Turns out that I don't actually love someone trying to hack my brain."

CHAPTER 16

The girls returned and Belle had calmed down, but they crawled into the front of the van while Moss lay on one bench with Zip opposite him, working away. Moss was relieved that he didn't need to go into the program for Zip to do his thing, but he was bored and found himself dozing off.

He felt himself enter a half-dream. He was not fully asleep but knew he wasn't awake either. He was vaguely aware of the van as he pictured himself on a beach with Issy, looking out over the ocean. He could hear the lapping waves and smell the salt air. He had always wanted to spend time at the ocean but hadn't yet had the chance.

Stan had kept saying they were going to go back in Moss's early days with the crew, but they never made it. There was always some restaurant to try or some job to run.

In his mind, it was a beautiful day at the beach and he dug his feet into the sand, curling his toes. He could almost feel it, just out of reach at the tip of his mind.

He didn't know if he had actually fallen asleep, but his eyes shot open as Zip exclaimed, "No shit!"

"What?" Belle and Ynna said in unison.

"Jinks," Belle giggled to Ynna.

"Huh?" Moss groaned.

"The breaker they got on you," Zip said. "Glyfph. I would never have figured them working for one of the megas, but here we are."

"You can tell?" Moss asked. He knew next to nothing about breaking.

"Took a while, but there are signs," he said. "I'm going to try and get a location on them but I don't know if I have the skills."

"I believe in you," Belle called from the front.

Zip smiled but said, "It's not a matter of belief. I'm literally going up against one of the greatest breakers in the world."

He was clearly working on multiple fronts at once. One of his eye plates had gone dark, and he was typing with one hand on the tablet while manipulating something else being projected into the cab.

Sweat formed on Zip's brow and streaked down the black glass in his face. Moss turned to watch him as he heard a ringing sound fill the cab.

"Whaddup?" Moss heard Patchwork say.

"Know you are busy, but could you take a break and look at something?" Zip asked. "Sharing now."

"Heard," Patchwork said, and Moss felt like it was almost too on the nose.

The two breakers spoke in a language that was technically English but which Moss did not understand. He tried to pay attention and could tell that Ynna was also trying her hardest to follow along.

"Yes!" Patchwork and Zip Thud yelled in unison, Zip even thrusting his hand in the air in triumph.

"Thanks, brother," Zip said.

"My plez" Patch said. "Looking forward to meeting you IRL."

"Back atcha," Zip said, ending the transmission. He turned to Moss. "We got a lock on the location."

Moss grimaced. "Some fucking fortress?"

"Not even. A super swank villa north of the burbs in LeMario — the wealthiest part of North Mento."

"Really?" Moss asked in surprise. "You're telling me that they just have one breaker on me and it's not even in a secure location?"

"Looks that way," Zip said. "But you have to realize, if this is one of the best, they are going to have some protection."

"Naturally," Moss said. "Any idea who hired them?"

Zip shook his head. "Of course not."

The sky began to blue slightly as they drove toward the northern part of the city. The air warmed and the fog melted into clear night. The towering buildings began to appear in clusters rather than an endless sheet. The homes here were palatial with tall walls, though many had adjacent staff apartment complexes where the poverty abutted the wealth. The houses were of different styles to match the owner's taste, though all were modern interpretations. Moss couldn't help but gawk at the updated Tudor or ranch-style homes, the contemporary Victorian and Adobe. These sprawling palaces were so close to the people living in mounted coffin-style apartments and yet were a world away.

"It really pays to be one of the world's greatest breakers, eh?" Moss said as the van slowed in the morning traffic. Many people commuted from the main city center to the smaller outskirt districts for work.

Zip's head was resting against the window, his face tilted out. "I guess," he murmured. "I've never known this wealth."

"Guess you've been doing it wrong," Ynna joked.

Zip just nodded, the skin of his forehead sliding up and down the window. "Guess so," he said, not taking the joke.

"Have you been able to bring up schematics of the house?" Moss asked.

"No," Zip said absently. "There was a flag on the file that I couldn't get past without Glyfph knowing I was looking. But we can check it out from public world view."

He opened his tablet and projected the estate. Moss just laughed at the opulence of it: three stories of white marble façade with stylish black metalwork, squared angles and huge windows looking over an Olympic-sized swimming pool complete with hot tub and water slide. The pool house was larger than Moss's hex and the outdoor barbeque area had a bar, serving area and table large enough to seat ten. It was walled off and Moss could see security cameras, but at least from the public view, there were no additional security measures.

"A person lives there by themselves?" Belle asked in shock, her hands dangling over her seat as she looked back.

"Lucky, right?" Zip said. All the wealth on both sides of the road seemed to have really hit him hard and turned him into a sulky teen. Moss knew he would need to snap out of it if they were going to have any luck with the breaker.

"Not really," Belle said, and Zip turned to look at her.

"I mean, look at these places," he said, a whiny overtone hanging on the words. "One of them could house my entire family, extended family and all their friends. The amount of money anyone who lives here makes in a day, in an hour, could probably feed a whole block for a year."

"So what?" Belle asked.

"So what?" Zip asked in mock impression. "Wouldn't you want that?"

Belle looked at him pityingly. Moss couldn't help but feel the expression was perfect.

"No," she said flatly. "I would rather have you in a shabby apartment than all this and no one."

Zip seemed to consider her words and Moss smiled. That was love. Designed and programmed, but love nevertheless. He was amazed by the realism of it. It was a machine, just a really high-tech toy, but it had just expressed feelings as true as Moss had ever seen.

Zip gripped one of the mounted straps and pulled himself forward toward Belle. Moss slid toward the rear of the van to give him space behind the passenger seat.

"Really?" he asked, and Moss just watched in amazement. He could see Ynna stealing glances as well.

"Of course," Belle whispered sweetly as she grabbed his hands in hers. "Wouldn't you?"

"Yes," he said.

"We do not need all this,." She nodded in the direction of the houses, now glinting gold in the morning sun.

"No," he agreed. "We have everything."

They began to kiss, softly at first but with a growing intensity. Ynna lay on the horn for a moment and they pulled apart.

"Sorry," Ynna lied. "Some asshole cut me off."

"Fibber," Belle said with a clever little smile.

Zip looked apprehensively at Moss who asked, "What's up?"

"Can we, like, stop for some food?"

Moss laughed. "Sure thing, why wouldn't we?"

Zip shrugged. "I don't know, I've never been on a secret mission before."

"Me neither," Belle said, raising her hand. Ynna covered her mouth with one hand to keep from laughing.

"Better if we just do drive-thru," Ynna said, merging right toward an exit. "Back Burger, anyone?"

They picked up their fast food, pulled into the parking lot of the restaurant and ate in silence. Once everyone was finished and complaining about eating too much, Zip looked at Moss.

"So, like, how do we do this?"

"Shouldn't get violent. I would really just like to talk to the person, find out who they are working for," Moss said, trying to make it sound far easier than it was.

Zip narrowed his digital eyes. "I don't understand. Your plan is to just go up to the person being paid to find you and talk to them?"

Moss had to think a moment. "Well, it sounds dumb when you say it like that."

"Probably because it is dumb," Ynna said into the open doors from behind the van. She zipped up some coveralls from the footlocker and continued. "We will go out there and get the lay of the land. If it makes sense to go in, we will, but we won't make any decisions until we see it. The earth view may have looked unguarded but there is no way in hell it actually is. I'm sure they just hacked the system to make the house look like it did on the market rather than how it looks now."

"That's what I would do," Zip agreed.

"Just another couple of minutes up the road to LeMario," Ynna said. A few wispy clouds pulled across the warm blue sky now and the day looked to be a nice one.

After just a few moments of driving, Sandra's voice materialized in Moss and Ynna's heads. *Status report?*

Found out who's trying to break into my brain, Moss informed his grandmother. *Single breaker but a good one, maybe one of the best. We are headed there now.*

Backup? Sandra asked.

Nah, Moss told her. *I think we may have too many already, actually.*

Copy, Sandra said. *Anything else?*

Get Tek out to where we were and have this kid's stuff brought to you, Ynna said. *He and his girlfriend are moving in.*

Patchwork vouched for him, but does the girlfriend seem okay? Sandra asked and the suspicion was clear in her words. They were trusting a new person very quickly and Moss knew his grandmother well enough to know that it would take a while before she trusted Zip.

Nothing to worry about on that front, Ynna told her.

Copy, Sandra said again. *Keep us updated and let us know if y'all need the cavalry.*

The communication ended as Ynna pulled down a tree-lined street where beautiful cars were parked just inside fenced-off, even more beautiful homes. Cameras were everywhere in this community and drudges embossed with neighborhood watch logos patrolled the street. These robotic guards were among many perks provided by the housing authority that owned all the houses and ran the area.

Ynna pulled off the road and parked just up a little hill from the target's house.

"Can you get anything from here?" Ynna asked as Zip pulled out his tablet.

"I'll try," he said as Ynna pulled out binoculars to examine the house. Moss climbed forward into the passenger seat beside her.

"See anything?"

"No," she said. "That's what worries me."

"Yeah," Moss agreed. Only the top two floors were visible from the street and the blinds were drawn in all the windows. "There has to be more to it, right?"

"Yes," Ynna said without a shred of doubt. "What's our play?"

Moss stared at the house. If he hadn't known that there was something unusual about it, there would be no way to tell. It was simply another gorgeous house in a fine neighborhood. Some leaves danced up the street in a slight breeze.

"There it is," Zip said, staring at his tablet.

"Where what is?" Belle asked.

"The house is a fortress, but not the way we suspected," he told them. "I didn't find any armed guards or anything like that, but there is a DataRampart around the whole place and everything is on two backup generators. If anyone with anything controlled by electronics passes through their mesh, Glyfph will control it. That chip they're working on breaking," Zip pointed to Moss's head, "you may as well just hand it over. That hand," he said, pointing to Ynna's obvious cybernetic, "all theirs."

"Shit," Moss said.

"Yes and no," Zip informed him. "I can run a counter on it, but I'll need to stay right beside you and it's risky."

"Think you could keep it up long enough for us to get close?" Ynna asked.

"I think so," Zip said, but his voice betrayed him.

"You sure you are okay with this?" Moss asked.

Zip shook his head. "No, not really," he admitted. "But a deal's a deal."

"Those had better be some fucking hands," Ynna whispered to Moss.

"What should I do?" Belle asked.

Zip reached up, putting his hand on the nape of her neck. "Why don't you take a little nap," he suggested, his finger vanishing behind her ear.

"Okay," she said. "I love you."

He smiled at her. "I love you, too."

Her eyes closed and her true nature was betrayed by the sound of her system shutting down with the low hum only a machine makes.

Zip turned and they discussed the plan, looking at the structure and trying to come up with every possible outcome and eventuality.

The young man's hands were shaking when he finally said, "Okay, let's do this."

CHAPTER 17

"You're putting a lot of faith in someone you hardly know," Ynna noted quietly to Moss. Zip was getting ready, taking a few deep breaths before they walked down the hill.

"I trust him," Moss told her. He did. He had only known the kid a very short time, but he could sense that he was good. Moss knew to trust his instincts.

Ynna shook her head, her face worried. "I trust him too, but that doesn't mean he's up to this."

"What other choice do we have?" Moss asked, wishing she would give him a good answer.

"Just have Anders fly over here and I'll blow the fucking place to smithereens with a rocket launcher. Or we drop grenades on the place. Or crash a car full of C4 into it."

Moss held up his hands. "I get the picture," he said. "But I need to ask them who they are working for."

"Why?" Ynna asked sincerely. "It's either Carcer or ThutoCo; what difference does it make?"

Moss felt his stomach knot and his jaw clench. "You have someone try to literally hack your brain and then tell me it doesn't matter who."

Ynna sighed. "Alright, I hear you. This whole thing just worries me."

"Me too," Moss admitted.

Zip trotted over. "Okay," he said and once again, he looked like just a child. A head shorter than Moss and Ynna, the little beanpole did not inspire a great deal of confidence. But Moss knew he was good. All he had to do was keep the dampener up long enough for them to find Glyfph and they would be fine.

Zip had his tablet out and worked as they moved, narrating what was happening and what he was seeing with his eye plates.

"Establishing graymaker now," he said. "Stay close to me. The bubble is tight. I can see it, so I'll let you know if you are getting too far, but don't make me. Try not to talk too much as we move but verbal communication is going to be key here."

Moss raised an eyebrow and Zip answered the question. "Neural comms are just another form of data that could raise their awareness of us. They probably have a lot of sounds in the room, or they are actually synched with, or socketed into, their computers, so real-life sounds are actually safer."

Moss saw Ynna give a little smile; she was impressed with the kid.

They moved as one toward the yellow wall with vines growing in patches around and over it. Ynna slid up against it, interlacing her fingers and bending at the knees. She nodded to Moss who used his cybernetic legs to hop over the wall in one fluid movement while staying as close as he could to Zip.

Moss lifted the young man who awkwardly threw his weight over the wall. Moss reached up to help him down, keeping an eye on the camera as it began to slowly glide back to face in their direction. Moss didn't know how much the breaker was paying attention to his security cameras, but he did not want to find out. Ynna hopped down and the three crept along a low bush line toward the house.

The sun was bright and Moss wished they had made it in time to do this at night despite Zip's suggestion that the early morning might be the one time they might catch Glyfph sleeping. "Breakers tend to keystroke all night and go down when the sun comes up," he had explained. Moss hoped he was right. He knew better than to expect an easy mission, but he always liked an optimistic outlook.

They moved silently toward the house. Large sliding glass doors faced a little seating area under the second story which jutted out as an awning. Paved with fine tiles, the area held a couple of wicker chairs with moldy cushions that suggested they had never been used. Zip held up a hand and got to work on the camera pointing to the seating area, putting it on a loop.

He gave a thumbs up and they moved forward. Moss's already-racing heart nearly pounded through his chest as he saw the wet footprints they were leaving on the tiles. He reminded himself to breathe as his eyes darted around, waiting for some surprise — guns popping out from the bushes, an army of drudge guards, anything.

This was all feeling too easy. "Some breakers think they are too smart to get attacked," Zip had suggested and, once more, Moss hoped the kid was right.

Ynna knelt by the locking mechanism and manually broke into it. The tip of her robotic hand opened and she stuck it in the side, letting it work. The moment seemed to take forever. A bird trilled and the quiet swish of a sprinkler waking up on some distant lawn started. If not for what they were doing, it was actually a lovely day in a nice place. The smell of freshly cut grass filled their noses and the choking pollution of the city was replaced by clean, light air. Moss took a deep breath, letting the oxygen sink into his lungs.

The door beeped and the moment passed. Ynna moved slowly toward the door, sliding it open. The interior of the house was as beautiful as the outside. White walls displayed fine art and sculptures. Paintings of robed figures amongst ruins surrounded them, illuminated by natural light from all sides. The open floor plan allowed for visibility in all directions and Zip once again got to work on the cameras. A large kitchen area with bar countertop lay to their left and straight ahead was a couch facing a fireplace large enough to pull a car into. Zip pointed right toward a staircase.

They started upward, the thick, soft white carpet squishing under Moss's boots. He held his Kingfisher tight against his thigh as he moved. At the top of the stairs was a large podium with a glass case on the top. Within was a white marble hand gripping a clump modeled to look like clay with figures emerging from it.

The sculpture was stunning, and Moss tried to reconcile this home with what he knew of breakers. He understood that not all people were the same, but this place lay in stark contrast to every single computer expert Moss had ever met.

There was as little movement upstairs as there had been downstairs. It was quiet and still. There were more paintings and a lot of closed doors. Zip nodded down one hallway and they moved toward it. Ynna looked around nervously, a bead of sweat streaking the side of her face.

It was a strange relief to see the large, incongruous metal door at the end of one long hall. It had felt as if they were in the wrong place and seeing something with that level of security finally fit. Even though Zip had hacked the cameras staring down at them from the door, they were still ominous as

Ynna moved forward toward a keypad and tried her hand at breaking in but she shook her head.

Zip gave it a try on his tablet, his hands looking like hummingbird wings. But he too shook his head. Moss attracted Ynna's attention and pointed to his legs. She nodded. Moss looked at Zip who also gave a nod, though his was in defeat. Moss stood, backed up and moved forward to kick in the door with his cybernetic leg. The pistons would fire and the metal would make short work of the door.

"That's quite far enough," a voice said through a speaker system. Moss stopped dead. Zip and Ynna looked terrified.

The ground rushed up to meet Moss but he didn't feel himself hit the floor.

He opened his eyes in his hex.

Standing from his bed, he rushed over to his computer but it wouldn't turn on. Glyfph had gotten in. Ynna had been right; they had walked directly into a trap. The kid was good but not good enough.

"Finally," a voice cooed in a South African accent and Moss turned, knowing exactly who he was about to see. "I will never understand why you are making this so difficult," Arthur Smith, President of ThutoCo, said. He was perfectly digitally recreated in the program. His salt and pepper hair, fine suit and shark's smile were all there.

"This time, I know exactly where you are," Arthur said. Moss hammered his computer, trying again and again to call for help.

Arthur Smith shook his head. "Won't work. I have you this time."

"No," Moss said, trying to convince himself that it wasn't true. He knew BurbSec would already have been dispatched. He tried to reach out to Ynna in his mind; maybe she was close enough. He felt a tickle. She *was* close.

"But, really, Moss, why are you making this so hard?" Arthur asked. "Why not just come to us, let us take the chip and live a normal life?"

"Because you are evil," Moss said. "You killed my parents, and you will kill me."

Arthur shook his head and poured himself a drink in a square glass. Moss hated that the man was moving so easily in a program within his own mind.

Moss focused, closing the eyes to his mind while he looked at Smith in the program.

"I did not kill your parents. We did not kill them," Arthur said, swirling the drink and watching as the liquid ran back down to the bottom. "Their actions killed them," he continued. He was stalling and Moss knew it. Arthur had the upper hand and was just wasting time until his people could arrive.

But Moss could use the time. In a vision like a dream, he accessed the screen. The monitor wasn't real; none of it was. It was all his to control. He fought hard to see the screen in his mind, to work and press forward. The counterprogramming was strong, but Moss kept working. He brought up the security code.

He could do this.

He saw a flicker in his vision as Arthur kept talking, smirking and being condescending. Moss saw a screen superimposed before Arthur. It was the feed from the camera. He saw his body lying on the ground as Ynna slapped him and Zip screamed for answers.

Get Glyfph! Moss transmitted to Ynna and he used all his might to control the program.

The door to the room opened. He saw Ynna look up and smile.

Then he felt the punch.

"No!" Arthur Smith howled and hit Moss in the face. It hurt as the program told his brain it was being punched. Moss fought to keep the vision but he lifted his hands as Arthur did the same. They circled one another.

Arthur struck out again but Moss deflected, trying to focus both on the fight and switching the security cameras.

As he did, Arthur Smith lunged, knocking Moss to the ground as he watched Zip and Ynna enter a room. It was not like those of other breakers Moss had seen. It was three simple monitors sitting on a desk. Ynna lifted her machine gun as she entered.

"Wake him up!" she demanded, pointing the weapon at the leather chair.

Moss's heart stopped when the chair turned. Arthur struck and straddled him as Moss watched the moment unfolding. He felt the pain and knew he was being attacked in the program but didn't care.

Ynna's eyes went wide and began to well the instant she saw Rosetta.

Moss recognized her instantly. She had been their hacker when he had first joined the crew and had died before their very eyes. Moss knew there was more of a history between the two of them than Ynna had ever let on.

"No," Ynna murmured, the heartbreak clear as day.

"You left me," Rosetta said, her half-tattooed face hard and cold. "You left me there to die."

"But you *were* dead."

"I may as well have been," Rosetta said, "for the way I was treated."

"No," Ynna said again.

Moss tried to reach out to her, but the image crackled and wiped out as Arthur continued the barrage. Within the program, Moss could feel his face swelling. Moss closed his eyes and the pounding stopped.

"This is my program," he said. "My father's program, my mother's program. *My* program."

At that, Arthur began to rise into the sky. His hands locked to his sides as if controlled by magnets.

"This program will not control me," Moss said. "I will control it."

"We are coming!" Arthur screamed before turning into static. He jerked and contorted unnaturally.

"I am in you!" he shouted before vanishing. Moss fell to the ground. He focused. He needed to stand, needed to get out of the program.

It's not real! he tried to tell Ynna, but he could tell the communication was failing. He opened the security feed again.

"When you left me, I turned to people I knew would help me," Rosetta said. "ThutoCo took me in, helped me when you abandoned me."

Moss had told all of them about the android copies, but the trick still worked.

Rosetta had died. Moss had watched her die.

But in that moment, Ynna couldn't see past the fact that her old friend was standing before her.

"I'm so sorry," Ynna wailed, letting her weapon drop. "I'm sorry I let you die, I'm sorry I brought you into this life. I'm sorry for all of it."

It's a fake, Moss tried to warn her. *They are just trying to keep you busy!*

Ynna didn't hear him.

He was exhausted. He tried to leave the program again but had expended too much energy.

"You should be sorry," the Rosetta facsimile said, standing from her chair. She looked just as she had in real life, short with a sweet smile and hieroglyph tattoos.

Moss tried something different.

ThutoCo is coming, he explained. *This person is not real. She is just an android, a copy of someone we used to know. Kill her so I can be free.*

Moss saw Zip Thud's head tilt. He had heard Moss. Somewhere in some program in his mind, he had gotten the message.

"Moss says she's a copy," Zip said.

"She can't be," Ynna wailed, but Moss could hear the doubt.

"I'm real," Rosetta said.

We don't have time for this! Moss tried to reason. Zip pulled out his gun, aiming it in a hand so shaky that Moss doubted he could hit her even at such close range.

"Please," Rosetta begged, holding up her hands. She was unarmed and beginning to cry. The performance was working on both Ynna and Zip and above all, she was stalling for time. Rosetta wailed, "I am real."

Moss thrashed against the program. He needed his body. He needed to get them out of there before ThutoCo arrived.

"I can't do it," Zip said. "Even if she isn't your friend, she *is* real."

Moss wanted to scream, "No she isn't," but he knew how Zip felt about androids. This argument was lost before it began.

"How did we meet?" Ynna asked, raising her gun again, but before she got her arm halfway up, Rosetta speared her to the ground. The machine overpowered Ynna quickly and Zip just stood in horror. Blood sprayed the room as Rosetta slit Ynna's lip, cracked her jaw and broke her nose.

Moss watched in horror.

Zip raised the gun, a tear rolling down his cheek.

Rosetta was blasted sideways as she was shot in the side. Blood, or whatever the makers used for blood, splattered everywhere. Ynna coughed and sputtered. Moss reached down to help her up.

Watching her being beaten had been enough to break him free and he had run over just in time to watch the scuffle.

One of her eyes was swollen shut and she looked as miserable as he'd ever seen her.

"Fuck them," she said, blood pouring down her chin as she spoke. "Fuck them for this."

They both turned to look at Zip, who was frozen. He blinked, seeming to see them for the first time, and vomited. The smell filled the room and Moss gagged as the chunky brown liquid sprayed all over the computers. Zip bent at the waist and put his hands on his knees before throwing up again.

His face was pale and he wiped his mouth with his sleeve.

"We have to get out of here," Moss said, but he wasn't sure how far they could get in their respective states.

"Employee Moss," he heard projected on a loudspeaker from outside the house. "Come out with your hands up."

Moss's heart sank. "Fuck."

CHAPTER 18

"For violating corporate policy, your non-disclosure agreement and taking company property off site, we have been authorized to detain you," the voice said.

Ynna and Zip looked defeated. Ynna didn't even seem to care anymore. Seeing Rosetta killed again had taken too much of a toll on her psyche. The violence had been too much for Zip. This had not been his fight and he couldn't take it.

"It's fine," Ynna said, moving limply out of the room as she sprayed some healing solution on her face. "I called Sandra for backup before we came in here."

"You did?" Moss asked, more than a little offended.

You on your way? Moss heard Ynna ask.

Nearly there, Anders informed them.

Moss was so relieved that he couldn't even be upset that Ynna had ignored him.

You've got company, Anders informed them.

Moss shook his head. *We know.*

You know Carcer is en route too? Moss's heart sank even further. This was too much. Looking at the battered and beaten Ynna and psychologically wounded Zip, he knew they were in trouble. They made their way to a window, looking out to see a unit of BurbSec Zetas, ThutoCo's elite soldiers.

Ynna turned a now-purple and yellowing face on Moss. "I'm getting pretty sick of this view."

"You and me both."

You guys just sit tight a moment, Anders suggested.

They all crouched, periodically peeking over the sill to watch the Zetas. Dressed in their white plate armor over grey mesh bodysuits, they were getting into position with their weapons aimed at the building. Their helmets were down, slitted face shields glistening in the sun. Moss was relieved to see there were not that many actual soldiers but didn't like waiting while Carcer was sending people of their own.

Ynna was right. Being surrounded, on the defensive, was getting really old. Moss was ready to take the fight to them. He was ready to get out of here and install the communication device so they could get the help they needed to actually bring the battle.

He knew there was a long way to go. They still had to wake up the citizens, arm them and show them that there was more to the world. They had to deal with Carcer, ThutoCo and the entire AIC. But they would.

At least, he thought, they would if Anders could get them out of here.

Another BurbSec officer sprinted out of the bushes. Moss wondered if there were many more he couldn't see. He ducked back down. Ynna was trying to wipe the blood off her face with her sleeve, but it was a slow process and she only managed to smear it all over her face in a grisly display.

He turned to Zip. The kid's face was tilted up and he seemed a million miles away.

"How you holding up?" Moss asked.

It took a moment, but Zip turned. His chin was streaked with drying vomit. "Um," he said as though he was searching for words that were far away. "Not so good." He emphasized each word carefully and slowly.

"Yeah," Moss said. "I'm sorry I got you into this."

"Guess we can call it even," Zip said with a morose smile.

Moss sighed out a laugh. "Right."

"So, this is, like, your whole life?" Zip asked.

"Pretty much," Moss told him.

Zip shook his head slowly. "Think I may want to cancel the movers," he joked without any levity.

"I can appreciate that," Moss admitted. "But it won't be like this for you. You'll hang back, work with Patch, spend your nights with Belle. It'll be good."

"Okay," Zip said softly. "I know she would like to be around people more. She's always on my ass to go out with friends. But it's like . . ." he got cut off.

"Employee Moss, I repeat, we have you surrounded," the voice boomed again. "Turn yourself in or we will be forced to take . . . " but now the voice was cut off. It made a loud gurgling sound into the loudspeaker, which whined with feedback and shut off.

The three readied their weapons and peeked over to see a knife being pulled from the neck of the Zeta who had been threatening them. The weapon was being held by another ThutoCo officer. The Zetas were turning around.

One screamed as he was shot through the chest from a great distance, the shot ringing out from somewhere they couldn't see.

Coming in hot! Anders informed them just before the dropship appeared, moving fast.

Moss realized that Carcer wasn't taking any chance this time. Behind Anders, two flighted Carcer cars were closing in and opening fire. Shells rained down on the house as the ship blasted past. The wail of Carcer sirens began in the distance as well. Both companies were coming for them now.

One of the Zetas looked up as the ships screamed by. A bush moved closer to the Zeta. The man turned and was greeted by a blunderbuss shot to the face, blasting open his helmet like a watermelon hit with a hammer.

"Time to go," Moss said and the other two followed as he went first down the stairs. As he moved past a wall, a Zeta's arm darted out, clotheslining Moss's neck and causing him to fall to the ground. As he choked, he saw the Zeta move toward Ynna who moved with lightning reflexes.

She let out a barrage of shots into the man. The noise was deafening from that close a range and his armor sprinkled them with hot pieces as it shredded. More blood spewed and Zip screamed in horror, dropping his pointless weapon to cover his ears with his hands.

The body twitched and Ynna just looked annoyed as she reached down to help Moss to his feet. He tried sucking in air, but the gunpowder and smoke burned his swollen throat. He dragged Zip out toward the garden where Puck was standing with his bush camouflage, looking very pleased with himself.

Moss shielded his eyes, giving them a moment to adjust to the sunlight. He hadn't known the real sun for his whole life, rarely saw it in the city, and still had not grown accustomed to it.

"You lot appear to have been through the wringer," Puck said as they made their way out onto the grass.

"No shit," Ynna snarled.

Gibbs groaned as he pulled himself over the wall and landed with a thud beside a large, very heavy looking military bag. He rushed over to hug Ynna, who winced at both the touch and the public affection.

"Not the time," she said, pushing him away.

"I'm so happy you're all right," he said, then looked her over. "Well, alive, anyway."

"Thanks," Moss rasped.

Gibbs looked up. "You too," he said, but then turned back to examine Ynna's wounds, fussing over her.

"What's in the bag?" Moss asked, pointing to the green duffel.

Gibbs ran across the yard as more shots rang out from the other side of the wall. They all ducked but it didn't sound like they were coming in their direction.

"Anyone know how to use one of these?" Gibbs asked, pulling a rocket launcher with a computer targeting system out of the bag.

No one spoke and Moss, Zip and Steampuck looked at one another.

"I guess I have to do fucking everything," Ynna snorted.

As she took a step forward, the earth shook, and a piece of the wall exploded about fifteen meters from where they were standing. They all crouched and covered their heads before readying their weapons. Sandra stepped through the dust and crumbling wall with a BurbSec officer who was holding a bloody combat knife.

"What the fuck?" Ynna screamed in furious disbelief.

"Weren't going to climb some wall," Sandra said, shrugging.

The BurbSec officer ran toward Moss, the visor lifting to reveal Issy's face. He smiled as she hugged him. "I tried to stop her," she whispered of his grandmother.

Ynna spit a mouthful of blood, lifted the rocket launcher and knelt, bracing her body. Sandra pulled another, smaller model around from where it had been slung on her back and positioned herself as well.

Make another pass, Sandra commanded to Anders. Within a moment, the sound of approaching sirens was drowned out by incoming ships. Moss ushered the others inside just as Anders flew overhead. The ground vibrated as the ship moved so close to the ground that a beautiful painting crashed to the ground from the wall. Puck moved over to examine the work as Ynna and Sandra fired at the pursuing cars.

Plumes of smoke tailed the rockets toward the cars. Ynna's struck, causing a massive burst in the sky. Black smoke filled the air as what was left of the car crashed into some nice home in the distance.

The other car banked just in time, the rocket missing before detonating in the sky. Rather than continuing to follow Anders, the car now turned, firing forward-facing guns at them. Chunks of grass and earth spewed in every direction. Ynna and Sandra ran for the house as the car lifted and pitched to make another pass.

"To the roof," Sandra commanded, and they all ran up the stairs.

Chunks of wall erupted all around them as the car fired into the home. Ynna and Sandra were reloading while running but it was hard work and Ynna's eyes were now almost swollen shut.

Glass rattled and the Carcer car moved away, beginning to turn. Gibbs stopped halfway up the staircase, lifted his rifle to rest in the crook of his shoulder, took a quick breath and fired.

If Moss had been able to hear anything by that point other than a dull ringing, that shot would have pushed him to deafness. The massive bullet whizzed through the air and struck the car in the center of the rear-right thruster. It cracked and fizzled and instantly began to smoke. The other thrusters began to tilt and autocorrect, but Gibbs shot again.

The rear of the vehicle dropped out and the front thrusters caused the entire car to rock forward before plummeting toward the ground. The cab of the car filled with safety foam as it dropped onto a neighbor's lawn.

"Let's get to the roof," Moss said. Ynna and Sandra stopped their work. Moss patted Gibbs on the back.

They made their way to a balcony where Moss had spotted a ladder to the roof. Anders was already hovering low with the ramp down when they arrived.

They all climbed in, exhausted.

"No more of this," Moss said, and everyone nodded. "From now on, we are going to be in the driver's seat."

Everyone nodded again as they buckled in. The door began swinging up slowly, cutting off the sound of the approaching street cars.

"Wait," Zip yelled, working frantically to open his belts.

"What?" Sandra demanded.

"What about Belle?" he wailed.

Sandra signaled for him to sit down. "Patchwork is driving the van back already," she told the kid, who still looked nervous. She sat down next to Moss and strapped in. "It's a good thing one of you had the sense to let us help."

"I thought we had it under control," Moss said, his head dropping in disappointment with himself.

"That's the fuckin' problem, ain't it," she sneered, tapping him hard on the temple with her middle finger. "Maybe try and use this every now and again."

"I will," he said, slumping.

Despite her words, he was happy they had stopped the hacker. But he knew that if ThutoCo had sent one, they would send more

CHAPTER 19

The mood was low.

Everyone was tired and miserable.

Moss had hoped the meeting between Zip Thud and Patchwork would be a joyous occasion, but Zip was too damaged to do much more than find a room and lie down with Belle.

Gibbs had taken Ynna to their room to tend to her, and Issy had followed Moss to his but excused herself when they both realized they were lost in their own thoughts.

She made her way back several hours later, knocking on the door before stepping in. She was nursing something in a ceramic mug with UNT scrawled across it. Moss could smell the alcohol from across the room. There was no furniture to speak of, so she leaned against the wall until he patted the bed beside him. It was not a romantic gesture and Issy smiled slightly and sat.

"Hey," he said.

She nodded, took a sip and said, "Hey."

"You want to talk about it?" he asked.

She nodded again.

"We've all been there," he soothed. "Comes with this life. But it doesn't mean we have to like it. I know Gibbs will always struggle."

"You know," she said, "it didn't actually bother me that much. In cadet training, they teach you a lot of methods for compartmentalizing and justifying your behavior. Weirdly, it worked. Just not in the way they hoped."

"Yeah, I'm pretty sure ThutoCo didn't teach you those tricks so that you would be okay with killing their agents."

"I mean, that's just it," Issy said. "They were agents of something evil and that's what I reminded myself of."

Moss furrowed his brows. "But," he began, but she knew what he was going to say.

"It's different with the Zetas," she said. "Those of us in the actual burbs didn't know what we were doing but we were also localized, contained, so it kinda didn't matter. Or at least I'm telling myself that."

She paused and thought. Moss just looked at her, wanting her to have the moment.

"The Zetas are different," she continued. "They know they are agents of destruction, of violence, of villainy. That almost made me madder. Knowing that they know they are evil. I mean, they were happy to come and kill you for what? For some chip, some program *your* family made. It's sick.

"Don't get me wrong, sticking a knife in a human being's neck for the first time is something I'm going to have to grapple with for the rest of my life, but the guilt isn't sitting on me the way it does with Gibbs."

"That's all we can hope for, really," Moss said and put his hand on her back. He knew she was seeing it, feeling it in that moment. In spite of her claims, he knew she was feeling her actions in her heart. He wanted to distract her.

He stood and beamed down at her, reaching out a hand.

She looked at him quizzically. "You still want to?"

"Do you?" he asked.

"A date's a date," she said, taking his hand.

"Damn right," he said. "We can stay close by, but let's get out of here and out of our heads."

She choked down the rest of whatever was in the mug and set it down on the floor. They were both in street clothes and would fit right in.

"We're going out," Moss called down the hallway.

"Nobody cares," Ynna called back, her voice still sounding weak though she was clearly feeling a bit better.

They let the grimness of their lives fall away and practically skipped through the building as they made their way toward the hidden access point. The area was largely abandoned, but there were transients taking up residence all around. A gang had previously occupied their building, so very few people tried to sneak in.

It was only a few blocks from derelict and abandoned to occupied slum. The empty streets began to fill with people and garbage. Single dim streetlamps became large overhanging lights, neon signs and lighted storefronts. The stores were not traditional places designed for the purpose of selling. Rather, they were former homes, the garages of which were converted into open stalls. Where there used to be parking spots for cars, now there were tables, displays or bars. The sides or rears had locked-off stairs leading to the operator's abodes. Most of the buildings also had more haphazard housing constructed on top of the original structures.

It was a common sight — people simply making do with what they could. Spaces were converted from their original purposes and more housing tacked on wherever there was available real estate. If a person owned a house, it made sense to convert the garage from a space for a car they couldn't afford to a store front and rent out whatever crappy apartment they could construct on top. People were desperate but clever and the city was rife with places like this.

A group of people danced happily in front of an open garage bar with the door up. Others cheered from within or sat watching the Miners game.

"San Tung kiosk just ahead," Moss said, pointing to where the street opened up into a roundabout with the small restaurant in the center. "Some dry fried chicken to soothe the soul."

She clutched his hand in both of hers and gazed up at him cheerfully. "Oh, you know just how to talk to a girl."

He laughed, though he could still see the sadness behind her eyes. It would be a while, a long while, but that didn't mean they had to wallow in sorrow. Bar stools surrounded the open restaurant, covered only with a light triangular roof. A hole with a little cap was set in the center, allowing the billowing smoke from the cooktops and fryers out but no rain in. Several chefs cooked simultaneously, plating and taking payment as they moved fluidly through the space. They all wore striped pants, black tops under stained aprons and garish pointed circular straw hats with green lights running around the rim — a look no doubt foisted upon them by their corporate overlords.

Moss and Issy sat, both happy just to be out together.

"If you had told me ten years ago that this would be our first date, I'd have laughed you out of the room," Moss said, chuckling.

Issy grinned. "If you had told me ten years ago that we finally went on a date, I'd have laughed you out of the room."

A waiter walked over and pointed at them.

"Two DFC bowls with rice," Moss said and the man nodded, pulling at his whiskers with ungloved hands.

Issy looked at Moss in shock. "Ordering for me is a little presumptuous, don't you think?"

"Oh, shit, I'm sorry, it's just the best thing on the menu. I can call him back," Moss stuttered but Issy laughed.

"Literally never gets old," she said.

"Oh," he sighed.

She waved the cook back and hooked her feet in the metal bar at the base of the stool so she could lean over the counter. She whispered something in the cook's ear, and he nodded before ducking out of sight. Moss gave her a quizzical look.

She shot him a conspiratorial smirk. "You're not the only one who knows secrets," she said. "Lots of places, like even my dad's, have real meat hidden away for regulars or higher-paying customers. You thought you liked this before. It's going to be *even* better with legit meat."

Moss smiled at her. He had seen Stan do the same thing but had never known what to ask, so he had been stuck with vat meat since Stan had been killed.

"So," Issy said. "I never thought I'd live to see the day."

"What day?" Moss asked nervously.

Her eyes went wide with excitement. "The day Gibbs actually found a girl."

Moss smiled. "Ah, that. I know; who'd have ever thought?"

"I mean, hell must really have frozen over," she joked but quickly stopped giggling and added, "but he's also really grown up."

"I know," Moss agreed.

"I think he only quoted two movie lines all day when I showed up," she said with a coy smirk. "Ynna's really having a positive effect on him."

"They really do seem good for each other," Moss said. "In the weirdest way ever."

"They sure are different," Issy agreed.

"Just means they challenge each other. It's good."

"They both know it, even if Ynna isn't the type to admit it."

Moss smiled. "She's got a soft spot."

"I know. There is just a lot of tough exterior too."

"Survival necessitated that," Moss said and then grinned, excited to be sharing a tidbit with Issy. "She's going to have a decision to make soon …"

Issy read his face and got excited like she had when they were kids and he was holding on to a secret. "What?"

"What do I get if I tell you?" he asked coyly.

Rolling her eyes and holding up a fist, she said, "Not punched."

Moss chuckled. "You're no fun."

She shoved him on the shoulder and pressed, "What?"

"Gibbs showed me a ring," Moss said with the usual excitement of telling someone a secret.

"No shit!?" Issy exclaimed.

"Crazy, right?"

"Cra- cra- crazy is right!" Issy said, but Moss could tell she was excited for her oldest friend. "I would be so happy for him!" she said before adding, "if she says yes."

"That's a big if."

"Yeah. She also seems pretty upset right now. And not just about the beating."

Moss ran a finger along a crack in the countertop, all the joy of the moment gone in an instant as they returned to thinking about their fight. "It's fucking psychological warfare. There was no reason for ThutoCo to mock up a hacker and make her look like someone we knew who had died except to hurt us, to break us. I mean, to think they took her body just to replicate, it's sick.

"I doubt they had any idea that it would impact Ynna the way it has but still . . ." he trailed off, thinking about it. "They make these machines and they are so lifelike. They use this bastardized version of my father's technology against us. I'm so tired of it. Nothing seems real anymore. Between my brain and these androids, I feel like I'm lost down the rabbit hole."

Issy put her hand on Moss's. It soothed him a moment and he looked up at her. She didn't speak for a long time.

"And what's the deal with that new girl — Belle, I think?" she finally asked, breaking the silence and clearly changing the subject for Moss's benefit.

Moss couldn't help but be amused at the question. "Well, speaking of, she's a machine, too."

"Oh," Issy said, the light going on. She grinned at her friend and was starting to laugh even before the words left her mouth. "Try to keep it in your pants, then."

He put his elbows on the table and buried his face in his hands. He knew she would not let him live down sleeping with that relief aide version of her anytime soon.

"I'm sorry," she snickered, rocking sideways to bump his shoulder with hers. "I had to."

"Always the ball buster," he said.

"Meh, that's why you love me," she joked but as the words left her lips, the air seemed to be sucked from the street.

Time stopped and Moss grappled with what he could possibly say. Issy felt it too.

The clonk of two bowls striking the plastic countertop saved them and Moss choked out, "You have to try this, you're going to love it."

He winced at his own words, but she just smiled and said, "I can't wait."

They forked up their first bites, and Issy's eyes widened.

"This really is so good. But it's better with the real thing, right?"

Moss nodded vigorously. They made small talk and reminisced for a bit before finishing the meal. After paying, Moss asked, "Should we walk around a bit?"

"Holy shit," Issy said, stopping Moss dead in his tracks.

"What?" he asked, eyes wide.

"This is like a real date."

He sighed and his shoulders dropped. "Yeah," he said.

As she stood to move in close beside him, she laced her fingers through his. It was a small thing, but for Moss it was everything. They walked the dirty streets, surrounded by poverty and misery, blissfully unaware of it all. Moss's whole life was now dedicated to changing this world but in that moment, all he saw was Issy.

"So," she said in a tentative tone, and he could tell she was about to discuss something delicate. He worried that she was about to tell him they should just be friends. "You mentioned your brain earlier."

"Oh," he said. "That."

"Right," she said. "That."

They had known each other so long that she didn't have to actually ask.

"I don't even know," he said honestly, searching for the words. He reached up and absentmindedly rubbed the base of his skull with his free hand. "This thing in my head. I know how valuable it is. I know it means I can hack and affect change in a way I would never have been able to otherwise but. . . " He couldn't quite finish the thought in his own mind, let alone aloud.

"But?" she led gently as they turned to wander down a small alleyway fronted with small shops, lit with bulbs strung overhead instead of the relentless signage of the main street.

"But it's a lot," he said finally. "And look, I know I shouldn't complain and that I am able to do remarkable things for a good reason, but it's just so much. To know that people are trying to hack my brain. It's…"

"Fucking terrifying?" Issy smiled slightly.

"Exactly!" he said. "I have no idea what they could do if they got in. I mean, I just saw a vision of Arthur Smith and he threatened me from within my own mind. It's so invasive, makes my skin crawl.

"Our minds are the one thing that are truly our own and to know that others could have access to it and are trying to manipulate it … that's some next-level shit for some kid from Burb 2152."

Issy chuckled. "Pretty sure your just-some-kid-from-2152 days are well behind you."

Moss shrugged. "I guess you are right."

"You scared?" she asked, though they both already knew the answer.

"Yes," Moss said, and the admission felt good. "All the time. Of everything."

"Me too," Issy said. "But I was before I even joined up with you guys. Being out here, working in the city after living in the burbs, was a rude awakening for me. Dad took to it fine but I was just scared all the time. I mean, combat training certainly helped me feel safer, but still."

"But still," Moss agreed.

"Shouldn't be that way," Issy said, looking down the street. The shopkeepers all looked bored, staring into one screen or another. People littered the street, passed out or awake in a haze, some cocktail of drugs coursing through them. "That's the other reason I came. It wasn't just my aunt, my fear or wanting to see you. It's that this world genuinely does need to change. I don't know enough about The Great Pandemic to know how the world became like this, but I know enough to know it shouldn't be this way."

The comment tickled Moss's mind. "That's another thing I've been meaning to learn more about."

"What?" Issy asked.

"The plague," Moss said. "I think there is more there."

Issy laughed. "There seems to be more everywhere."

"Seriously," Moss said. "Anyway, you're right."

"About the world?"

"Yes. We will change it. We are getting closer. I know it."

"We start working with some of the colonies, we really are going to move closer," Issy agreed.

He stopped walking and spun her to face him. She looked up at him with clear, bright, dancing eyes. "I'm so happy you came," he said.

"Me too," she said, a little sheepishly, and looked away. "We should get back."

"We should," he agreed, putting a hand on her chin gently, feeling her body move toward his.

They kissed and the world fell away once more.

PART III

CHAPTER 20

Judy grimaced at Moss and Issy when they returned to the safehouse.

"If you lovebirds are done canoodling, we have shit to do," they said seriously. Their hands were stained black with grease and their old coveralls looked like a Rorschach test.

"I'll catch up," Issy said, knowing she wasn't a part of this.

Moss followed Judy through the dining room and into a room they had converted into a workspace. Tools, cables, bits of metal and objects Moss didn't even recognize cluttered the room. In its center sat the box that had caused so many problems.

Judy balled a fist and rubbed their eyes in exhaustion, wiping more grime on themselves. "So, we have it all set up, ready to go."

"Good," Moss said. "And the technician?"

"Patchwork found someone perfect. You and I are going to do the approach tonight. Now, really.

"Sounds like the guy Patch found is in deep shit and he should let us right in and up. We will place this in the array and Anders will reach out to his contacts."

"You make it sound so easy," Moss said with a smile.

"I'm not looking to die today," they said.

"Neither am I."

"Now that you have your girlfriend here," Judy noted in a tone that sounded angry but Moss knew to be pained.

"It's not like that," Moss said quietly.

"Okay," Judy scoffed.

Moss wheeled around. "I'm sorry, I said I'm sorry! I don't know what you want me to do. I loved him too. He's dead and it sucks but being mean to me isn't going to bring him back!"

Judy's face turned red. "You may have loved him, but you weren't *in love* with him. It was a loss for you all, sure, but you will never know what it was like for me."

"So, tell me!" Moss yelled, throwing his arms wide.

Judy just shook their head. "Just get yourself ready to go."

"Fine," Moss said, turning to leave. "Coulda just told me that when I walked in, but I guess you just didn't want to see me with Issy."

Moss stomped away, wishing things were easier with Judy. He really did care for them but it had always been hard. Stan had a way of calming them down and bringing out their tender side. Moss had no such skill.

He went to his room and began to dress for the mission. He put on his Dermidos under an all-black outfit, attached the dronepack, laced up his boots, holstered his gun and pulled on his long coat. He sighed, feeling the relentlessness of it all.

Issy had recharged him but now he needed to go once again. He was relieved that it was just going to be him and Judy, for as hard as it sometimes was with them, he was happy to give everyone else a break. He knew they all needed it as much as he did and was relieved that they would actually be getting it.

He made his way down the hall and knocked quietly on the door. It swung open.

"Hey, man," Ynna said, looking tired and bruised. She was lying on the bed Gibbs had set up for them. He had splurged to get them a Comph brand down comforter and Ynna snuggled up with Perro sleeping next to her.

Gibbs snorted from a chair beside the door. "Oh, you're up," he half observed, half asked.

"Yeah," Ynna said with a smile. "Great job staying awake and making sure I didn't choke on blood or anything," she rolled her eyes playfully.

"Shit," Gibbs said, sounding genuinely sad about failing at his job but he yawned and rubbed his face. "Sorry."

"You heading back out?" Ynna asked Moss, managing to shift positions without appearing to be in too much pain. Moss knew she was full to the brim with painkillers.

"Seems that way," Moss said, and her arm flopped out toward him with a thumbs up. Gibbs stood, patting Moss on the shoulder.

"Good luck," Gibbs said and grinned at Ynna mischievously. "Now get out of here so I make Ynna *feel* better."

"Oh, shit," Ynna said with a mixture of shock and delight, throwing back the covers.

Moss couldn't believe it. Gibbs was acting like the man he had always pretended to be back in the burbs. It made him happy to know that his friend could still surprise him.

"You like that?" Gibbs asked Ynna with an air of false arrogance.

"I did," she said, her swollen face now also flushed. "I never understand it, but I love you," she told him and Moss's mouth fell open. Gibbs stopped dead in his tracks.

He recovered quickly and smirked. "I know," he said, and Moss didn't think he had ever seen his friend so happy.

Gibbs turned to Moss, his smile taking over his whole face. "I've always wanted to say that!"

Moss simply smiled at his lifelong friend, overjoyed for him.

"I mean," Gibbs said, turning back to Ynna, "I love you too."

She shook her head and smiled. "Yeah, no shit."

She turned to Moss. "Now you, get," she commanded, waving her hand dismissively as Gibbs moved toward the bed. Moss began to step from the room and was closing the door as she called after him, "Don't die."

He laughed as he shut the door and said through the wood, "I'll try not to."

Another door cracked behind him. Puck poked his face out, wearing a monogrammed pajama set with matching robe.

"Good evening," he said with a nod of his head.

"Hey," Moss said. "How's it going?"

"Quite all right," Puck said. "Off you go once more?"

"Always," Moss chuckled, still reveling in the moment he had just witnessed. He was so happy for Gibbs. He could tell that Puck wanted to talk and he turned his attention to the man.

"Spot of tea?" Puck asked, swinging his door wide.

Moss looked down the hallway, knowing his mission awaited him. "Sure," he said and followed Puck into the room he had made his own. Moss's jaw dropped when he saw the setup. Puck had truly made the place his own. Moss had known the man had been scavenging and even had a few items smuggled to him, but his room looked like a museum.

Unlike the rest of them who had a cushion on the floor, Puck had a four-poster bed with draped linens and heavy blankets on a large mattress. Where the other rooms had exposed, cracked and rotted out walls, Puck had a patterned crimson wallpaper expertly placed on a patched wall and covered in art. Moss stepped on nails and splinters in his room, but Puck had a rug which covered nearly the entire floor.

Puck made his way to a small cooktop sitting on a small end table as Moss peered at the art hanging all around.

"I didn't even see you take this," Moss said, walking over to a small, framed painting of a group of men shoveling coal into a belching furnace. He had seen it in Glyfph's house but hadn't noticed Puck steal it.

"It's a masterpiece," Puck said, lifting the hot kettle and pouring the water into two fine cups on saucers. "Didn't reckon they would be appreciating it any longer."

"Suppose you're right," Moss said, taking the cup as it was handed to him and blowing the steam from the surface.

"Moss," Puck said, standing a little too formally for Moss's taste.

"Yeah?"

"Today made me realize something," Puck announced.

"What's that?"

"I told you long ago that my sister was the true mastermind behind our operation, did I not?"

"You did," Moss said, finally taking a sip of tea and instantly regretting it. His lips burning as the water brushed them.

"Well, today reminded me that the life of action and heroism may not be my calling. I would still desire a place within the ranks, but away from the flight of bullets and all."

Moss lifted and dropped his head slowly. "Sure," he said. "I imagine we can come up with something, but you have to understand that you will sometimes be called on to fight. You may not like it, but you *are* good at it."

"It is a great tragedy of life to excel at that which you disdain or are miserable at rather than that which gives you joy," Puck said with a self-satisfied smile. It was always obvious when the way he phrased something pleased him.

"You're not wrong," Moss said, thinking about the words.

"I'm rarely wrong."

"I should be going."

"So soon?"

Moss laughed to himself. He knew he would never really get used to Puck's style. "Yes," he said, taking a sip from his cup before setting it down on a dresser — much to Puck's chagrin. "I'll think about what you said."

Moss left the room and walked down the hallway. This time, his grandmother was waiting for him in the dining room, leaning against a blue painted wooden counter with a door hanging open on a single hinge.

"I'm gonna drop you two to meet the mark," she told him, dropping a cigarette to the linoleum floor and stamping it out.

"Okay," Moss said.

"Heard some raised voices. Don't want no shit."

"I know. There won't be any."

"Best not be."

Moss's anger flared. "I just said there won't." He was not sure why her comment had needled him, but it had.

"Don't sass me," Sandra said, stepping forward.

Moss was tired, sick of being talked down to by her. He knew she was trying to help but her style was getting to him.

As he opened his mouth to speak, Judy said, "Let's go."

They held the case with the communication device under one arm. They had swapped their coveralls for purple pleather pants split down both sides and stitched together with bright green thread. Their tight top was a material Moss didn't recognize, with intersecting lines running all along it in pulsating different colors. The sleeveless top exposed Judy's patterned tattoos. Moss had never learned what the tattoos meant to them, only that they had gotten them in Hawaii before moving to B.A. City to work for Carcer.

Moss was happy they had cut the moment and the three headed out toward the van. The air was cool and crisp and wet with fog. It was dark in front of their building and Moss's eyes took a moment to adjust. Like pure sunlight, the dark was another thing he was still not used to.

Everything in his hex had little lights, meaning it was never really dark. Even at night, the halls were always illuminated by a low light. In the city, the night was as bright as the day lit as it was by the signs, projections and screens. The dark, the dark as it was here, was still very new to him.

"So," Moss said, the word leaving his mouth in a steaming plume. "Who is the contact?"

"Gambling junkie in deep," Sandra told him as she unlocked the vehicle. "At the casino now celebrating his daughter forgiving him for gambling away her college fund."

"Whoa," Moss said.

"That's grim," Judy agreed, looking at Moss with shared horror.

"No, it's opportunity found," Sandra corrected. "Piece of shit's our golden ticket."

"Sure, but still," Moss said.

His grandmother fired up the van and pulled out, heading back into the city. "Should be easy to recognize a white guy in sweatsuit in a predominantly Asian casino."

Judy clicked their tongue. "What makes it Asian?"

"The style, language and clientele. Don't come at me with that shit," Sandra huffed.

Judy shook their head, exhaling slowly.

"Name's Neil Keck, average height and build, glasses and hair styled in grease," Sandra continued. "Has a shift starts at five so you'll need to make contact and get him to give you access quick. Here," she said, and tossed back a credit chip. Moss caught it, turning it over in his hand. It was larger than the ones he was accustomed to and he assumed it was a more antiquated version that was harder to trace. "Once you are in and situated, pay him off. No loose ends with this."

Moss laughed. "Pretty sure they'll figure out it was us if they find this. Not too many people have tech stolen off the body of Alice Carcer."

"Don't mean we have to make it easier for them," Sandra said.

"And we don't want to give him any reason to be unhappy with us," Judy added.

Moss nodded and tucked the chip into a jacket pocket.

"Neil's apartment and den are within a block of his work, so he should be able to just walk you right over. He never leaves this small vicinity," Sandra said.

"Oh come on," Moss wailed in false misery. "This guy's life is really bumming me out."

"Yeah," Judy agreed. "Tell us something good."

Moss was happy to have this moment. He was pleased not to go into the mission feeling anger toward Judy.

Sandra just grunted. "Something good is that he's about to get richer, thanks to us."

"Lame," Moss said flatly, and Judy smiled in amusement.

The city became taller and brighter as they drove. Squat decrepit buildings became tenements, became apartment complexes, became high-rises. Carts pulled by people were replaced by sputtering cars belching choking fumes, were replaced by next-year's model. The city never seemed to end. Moss thought back to that night he had left the burbs, flying over B.A. for the first time, seeing the twinkling lights stretch endlessly in all directions.

Through tall office complexes, Moss could see the array structure flashing briefly in the distance. A tall black metal spire covered in satellite dishes loomed over an office compound. Even more massive dishes surrounded the structure on the ground. It was hard to get a good look but Moss did not like the idea of how high they would have to climb. He hoped they would not have to climb to the top but doubted he would be so lucky.

The streets grew louder as the numbers of bars, casinos, pill drops, strip clubs, whore houses, VR dens and every imaginable entertainment venue grew around them. Tourists and locals alike stumbled through the crowded streets with tall souvenir cocktails in hand. There was not a direction Moss could look where there wasn't an advertisement for a local attraction. Billboards, holoprojections and posters vied for attention, blaring information about this show or that. Celebrities hawked concerts, costume characters promoted venues where you could leave your children while you gambled or took in a show, and dancers, strippers and performers stood on every street corner to take at-cost pictures and get people into casinos. There were so many lighted signs and screens that the street was bathed in an unnatural light as bright as day.

Sandra pulled to a stop in a passenger loading zone behind several limos with doors flung wide open to let in or out their drunken clientele.

"Should be in there," Sandra told them, pointing to the open doors of the Dragon Lounge Casino Resort. Men and women, body-painted to look like scantily clad versions of terracotta warriors, stood by the door passing out vouchers. The ringing of gambling machines pierced the car door ceaselessly. The vehicle shook slightly as the red Chinese dragon statue that fronted the building shrieked and belched fire to the delight of onlooking passersby.

Sandra showed them an image of the man they were looking for. Moss and Judy nodded.

"I'll be nearby in case you get into a bind needs solving."

Moss shook his head. "Not this time."

Judy gave a quick nod of agreement. "We'll get this done clean."

"Good," Sandra said.

It was loud on the street. Everything seemed to make noise and the ground was sticky. Moss could see a streetcleaner bot making its way toward them, the little cube spraying disinfectant and water as it trudged along.

As they were about to step into the casino, Moss grabbed Judy's arm and they turned to look at him knowingly.

"Listen, before we go in," he started.

They smiled softly. "I know you are sorry, truly I do."

Moss relaxed a little. "I never meant to minimize your loss."

"I know it," Judy said, reaching out and giving Moss's bicep a little squeeze. "I'm sorry too. My emotions have always run close to the surface. You know that, but losing Stan made it so much worse.

"He was my person, my everything. We fell in love at the holidays like in some movie and it felt that way to me forever after. Losing him was the hardest thing that ever happened to me. My life was never easy, but he made it bearable. I feel like there is a hole in me that will never be filled."

Lights jumped against their face and glinted in their tearing eye. "You have to know that I don't blame you, but you have to give me some latitude. I'm sorry now and will continue to be but it doesn't mean that I won't go off sometimes and you just have to be fine with that."

"Sure," Moss said. "We are all frayed and you have more reason than any of us to be at your wit's end. I'm sure you wish you could have just stayed in the Mass Illusion."

"Sometimes I do, but I know it's for the best that you came for me."

"Yeah?" Moss asked dubiously as a crowd cheered inside the casino. The setting was incongruous with the moment, but neither of them seemed to care.

"Yes," Judy affirmed. "I was using the digital world as an escape from reality. I understand why there are so many digital junkies now. But it wasn't me, you know? I'm a fixer; I've always wanted, needed to repair what's broken. Hiding away, doing nothing, went against my nature, much as I liked slaying people in the arena rather than facing my own heartache."

"He'd be happy to know you are back amongst friends," Moss told them with a sad smile. The little bot moved around them as it whirred passed them up the street.

"I know he would. He would be proud to know we are making progress. He loved you, you know?"

Moss felt his face pull in with emotion. "I know. He became like an older brother to me."

Judy chuckled. "That's how he described it too."

They smiled at each other and Moss was happy they had cleared the air, though he knew they would be back at it in no time. To him, they really were all siblings.

"Let's go make him proud," Judy said and turned to enter the casino.

"Welcome, can I interest you in a game of pachinko?" one of the terracotta warriors asked, holding out a shiny slip of paper. "First game's free."

Moss kept walking but Judy snarled, "Eat shit and die, mega-slave."

Moss couldn't help but laugh. When all was said and done, he was really happy to have Judy back.

CHAPTER 21

They were met by rows of machines stretching away from them in both directions, flashing strobe lights, blasting techno, heavy cigarette smoke and bodies. There was not a single free machine as they moved deeper into the casino where there were gaming tables and sports books. Crowds were formed around a circle of descending seats looking down into a projection from The Flavium. People were making their bets as the competitors were eliminated live.

Moss scanned the faces but there had to be thousands sardined into this floor alone and he knew there were more above.

"How the hell are we going to find this guy?" he groused, and turned to see Judy having a similar moment. The stopped, just looking and realizing how difficult this was going to be. "Maybe Patch can hack the feed, do some facial recognition for us?" Moss suggested.

Judy shook their head. "If it was possible, he would have. Casinos are just about the hardest thing to break, up there with smart cars and homes."

"Oh," Moss said. "Well, I guess we keep walking and looking."

As they began to move again, a woman in a kimono stepped in front of them, holding out another slip of paper. "Stay four nights and get the fifth one free," she announced happily, her blond hair showing from under the black wig.

"I'm not staying in this appropriation factory a moment longer than I have to," Judy grumbled, blowing by the human ad and heading for the Komodo Café. Food was being served on a raised boardwalk above a glassed-off false beach replete with cloned Komodo dragons.

Moss did not want to think of how the animals must live so he turned to continue to scan for the man.

"Shit," Judy said, and Moss turned to follow their gaze.

He saw two large bruisers in suits hovering over a small person at a Conka machine. He couldn't get a good look at the person being intimidated, but the looming figures seemed as good an indication as any.

They began to make their way toward the figures. The two hulking men were dressed in fine suits and had ID badges indicating that they worked for the casino. One was shaved bald with a glistening head and a thin black beard wrapping down his face. The other had exposed, fine cybernetics that he obviously took great pride in.

Moss and Judy approached without looking like they were looking. They both turned and pretended to watch a machine while keeping tabs on the men out of the corner of their eyes. One of the bruisers shifted and Moss got a clear view.

"Of fucking course," he said when he laid eyes on Neil Keck.

"Nothing can ever be easy," Judy noted.

Moss moved a little to get a better view, jostling a woman at one of the machines. She wheeled on him and began yelling. He apologized in a whisper and moved away from her;

but when he looked back at the thugs, one was staring right at him.

He turned away but Judy was looking at Moss in disbelief.

"What should we do now?" he asked.

Judy shrugged miserably, glancing up to the ceiling. "There have to be at least twenty cameras pointed at them. No way we could make a move."

"Plus, with all these people, it would become a stampede," Moss said, looking at the sheer number of people all around. "Actually," he said, and started to move.

"What are you doing?" Judy hissed, following right behind.

"Uncle Neil!" Moss cried as he moved toward the three men. They all turned on him in shock and a few people cocked their heads before returning to their games.

Neil looked at Moss with utter confusion, but the two hired goons stepped back, allowing him space to pass. Moss knew that they could intimidate someone quietly and move them away from the floor, but as long as they were in public, the corporate men could not make a scene.

"How long has it been? Five, ten years?" Moss asked, moving toward the man. He furrowed his brows as though trying to actually remember Moss. "Don't tell me you've forgotten your favorite nephew, Jonathan," Moss said, flaring his eyes at the man, hoping he would pick up on it.

"Oh, right," Neil said, playacting terribly but going along with it. "Good to see you again, Jonny."

Moss frowned as he got closer. "I still don't like being called that," he admonished with a little laugh. The two security officers backed away a little further, cautiously watching the situation unfold.

"You remember my partner," Moss said, holding forth a hand as Judy strode over, looking impressed.

"Oh, um, sure, yeah," Neil stammered. Fear laced his words and he kept checking over their shoulders to the thugs.

"We were hoping to grab a bite," Judy suggested, pointing toward a restaurant where a woman dressed as a ninja was making sushi.

"Oh, right, sure," Neil agreed.

Moss turned to the thugs, who smiled false smiles and turned away.

They hustled him toward the restaurant. It was up a few low stairs and there were several empty tables. Neil was so rattled that he bumped his head into a paper lantern as they sat at the table. Moss sat across from him and Judy right beside, making the hint of a threat. He looked at them in shock.

"Who are you people?" he asked. He appeared to be only in his forties, but his face was weathered, eyes sunken, and his hair seemed to be coming out in patches. The sweatsuit he wore had copious unidentifiable stains and a sour smell. His fingers were calloused from too much play and the nails were short and cracked.

"We are the people who just saved your ass," Judy said.

"Yeah, no, I get that," Neil said. "But why?"

"We need something from you," Moss told him.

The man's whole body shook at the words and he laughed. It was a pained, sad sound. "I have nothing. Less than nothing. You think those assholes were there to congratulate me on my winnings?"

Moss looked over the man's shoulder to see that there were now more security guards watching them.

"We know you don't have money. That's not what we are after," Judy said.

"Really?" he croaked. He was jittery and absent. What little mind he had left was fed too little sleep and too many bright lights.

A ninja walked over. A tired voice came out of the mask. "What can I get you folks?"

"Sake and three glasses," Judy answered without looking up. "Bowl of rice for our friend, here."

The waitress jotted down the order in a tablet and asked, "Are you guests? Guests receive a ten percent—"

Judy held up a hand and the woman stopped talking, turned and left.

"We are here with an offer," Moss told the man.

"You never answered my question. Who are you?" Neil asked, his eyes flashing back and forth between them.

"We didn't answer because we have no intention of telling you who we are," Moss replied as a small bot delivered their drinks and the bowl of rice. Neil doused it in soy sauce and shoveled it in his mouth with chopsticks he didn't bother unwrapping from their paper case. Moss poured the warm drinks for everyone and he and Judy took sips.

"We need you to take us to your work and grant us access to the tower," Judy explained.

Neil squinted at them, dark sauce dribbling down the corner of his mouth. "Oh," he said finally. "That's who you are."

"Right," Moss said.

"I suppose you are going to offer to pay me off?" he asked sullenly. "Risk my job for a little money because you know I'm desperate? Take advantage of my condition?"

"Precisely," Judy said, pointing a finger and giving the man a little wink.

He looked down, the dark purple streaks under his eyes even more apparent. Then he seemed to have a moment of clarity and looked up at them with a little grin. "Okay, I'll take you to my work."

Judy slammed their ceramic cup down on the table and the man rocked back, nearly falling out of his chair.

"Listen friend, if you think you can sell us out to Carcer, you've got another think coming. For a start, Carcer only pays their own people bounties so dumbfucks like you don't try to take matters into their own hands. Next, we would never let you pull it off. What are you even thinking? Just find an officer on the street and tell him your little story? Lastly, I'm pretty sure that without our help, you are not going to leave here without some inverse kneecaps, if you take my meaning."

Neil sighed, rubbed his damp face, pushed the bowl out of his way and rested his head on the table. He didn't lift it as he said, "You realize that if we are caught, my job is just the first thing I will lose?"

Moss couldn't help but chuckle. "Guy, you seem to think you are in a stronger bargaining position than you are. Sure, we are asking you to do something risky, but we are offering you money and you were just being threatened. Like just a moment ago, remember?"

"I remember," he said into the table.

A long moment lapsed.

"Fine," Neil said in miserable resignation. "How do you plan to get us out of here?"

Moss looked at Judy. They shrugged.

Moss let out a slow sigh and closed his eyes.

"Hey, Moss," Judy said, holding up a hand to stop him. He opened his eyes again and looked at the dirty fingernails with chipped polish on Judy's rough hands. "I think you should take it easy on that cheat-code."

Moss agreed but said, "Yeah?"

"You depend on it too much and I know you think you have it figured out, but you really don't."

Moss nodded slowly. Neil looked at the two of them in baffled silence.

"You're right," Moss said. "And I don't feel like I understand it. Patchwork helped me to control it better but that's it. There is so much I don't understand or trust. I know my mom wanted to imbue me with a weapon, but I really feel like there is as much risk as reward. I have really come to learn that."

Judy smiled very slightly. "I'm happy to hear that you realize that," they said. "Let's be smart. Don't use that weapon they gave you unless you absolutely have to."

Moss felt relief wash over him. Whereas his own grandmother had forced him to use it, Judy understood that it was dangerous.

"I know you guys are talking English," Neil said, dipping his finger in the drink, tasting it and wincing. "But I have no idea what you are talking about."

"That's because this doesn't concern you," Judy said flatly. Neil pushed away the cup of sake. "Don't drink?" they asked him.

"Nah," Neil said before adding with judgmental overtones, "I never understood alcoholics."

Moss opened his mouth to point out the absurdity but Judy spoke first. "All right, we are going to get you out of here.

Once we do, you take us to the tower, let us do our thing and there will be a nice payday in it for you. Deal?"

"Feel like we already agreed to that," the man said, looking so exhausted that Moss didn't understand how he was even upright.

Judy just shook their head and turned to Moss. "Feel less bad having met him," they joked. "Should have suggested this sooner but it's a little dramatic: I've got an overcooker I can use to fritz a couple of the machines. That'll be our moment."

Moss smiled, happy to avoid using the program. Judy clicked the heel of their boot and a little arm popped out of the side. Under cover of the table, their actions would not show up on the cameras. They aimed a small pointer which they slid from their pocket and pointed at a bank of machines.

Clicking their heel again, a marble-sized metal ball rolled quickly toward the machines.

"Be ready," Judy said, and Moss grabbed Neil's arm, worried he would have to drag the man.

Nothing happened for a moment; then one of the machines began to ding wildly. The person seated began to cheer before a second machine went off and then a third. Moss pretended not to look at the guards but the moment they hurried over toward the commotion, the three were up and running.

Moss did have to drag Neil, who ran like a stumblebum, tripping and skidding through the flashing lights. The thugs did notice them and began to follow, but the assembled crowd made it impossible. One reached a cuff up to his mouth and Moss knew they would soon have company.

Luckily, they were close to the entrance. They slowed to a fast trot in order not to attract any more attention than they already had. They heard shouting as they left and made their way through the wide door and onto the street.

Judy guided them in a direction Moss had not expected — across the street and into another casino, this one Fantasy Elf themed.

"Different owners," Judy informed them. They made their way from one side of the gaming floor to the other and out another door onto the street, where they pushed through more people before repeating the process.

After a while, it was clear that they lost their pursuers.

Neil looked at the two of them with a mixture of fear and awe. "Can I keep you guys?" he said in a tone that made it clear he was trying to make a joke.

Moss didn't acknowledge it, let his face fall flat and pointed to the communication tower.

CHAPTER 22

"This is my cousin and his partner," Neil said. "I'm giving them a tour of my station and letting them out to take pictures of the city from Level 1."

The CommiTech security officer seated in a little room beside the gate nodded. She hadn't even bothered to shut off her lenscreen when they approached. She opened a key box, lifted out two visitor badges with bright orange lanyards and held them out.

"You'll tell them the rules?" she asked, obviously watching her show again.

"Yep," Neil said as they took their badges and hung them around their necks.

She pressed a button and the heavy metal gate began to roll open. They walked through. Standing directly at the bottom of the tower, Moss realized just how truly massive it was. He had to crane his neck to look at the top and could hardly see it from the ground at night. He could only vaguely make it out because of the flashing lights to keep vehicles from hitting it.

The space was open and dark, illuminated by only a few streetlamps between the security checkpoint and the base of the tower. It was quiet, with just one person walking to their car in a little employee lot off to the side of the field of massive dishes. The employee looked up as they got in their car and gave a little friendly wave to Neil.

"My cousin and his partner," Neil called, and the guy getting into his car gave a disinterested thumbs up before closing the driver's-side door.

"Don't overcompensate," Moss whispered. "Nobody cares."

Neil seemed almost unable to speak. His whole body was shaking and the profuse sweat was beginning to turn his clothes a dark gray.

"You need to calm the fuck down," Judy told him in a threatening voice while they walked toward the wide base of the tower.

"Fuck," Neil sputtered. "Has anyone ever calmed down when *ordered*?"

"Just take a deep breath," Moss suggested and he did, not that it had any effect. He jumped and shook when a nearby repair drone took off and buzzed toward the tower.

Moss decided to try a different tactic. "I thought this tower was owned by either Carcer or NeoVerge," he said in an inquisitive tone.

"Oh, no," Neil said, sounding clear for the first time since they had met. Moss realized that the man, before giving his life over to his addiction, had been a passionate communications officer. "CommiTech owns the building and the employees work for them. The communication bandwidth is rented by other companies. D2E had rented almost the entire array until recently when Carcer went into business with NeoVerge and began the interplanetary comm system. It was actually a really exciting time for me and my team, full of new challenges. It really kept us on our toes."

The life seemed to return to him while he spoke; his voice was light and excited and he wasn't freaking out. Moss smiled.

They walked to the building at the base of the tower. It was a normal, squat office building with a worn CommiTech logoed mat lying in front of sliding glass doors. Neil waved his badge and the door slid open. He kept talking about the tower and its history as they rode the elevator up to the top floor. They disembarked and made their way to a staircase.

They passed no one as they moved through the building and there was only one sleeping security guard on the wide roof. Metal pylons stretched into the dark sky and Moss stared in wonder at the massive structure.

"Obviously, the shape and style were modeled after the Eiffel Tower in Paris," Neil said, guiding them toward an open, wrought iron elevator at the center of the tower.

Moss paused a moment before stepping into the elevator. Both Neil and Judy paused to look at him. He took a slow breath and stepped in. Neil slid the folding metal door closed and latched it. The whole system was far too rudimentary for Moss's taste.

When the elevator lurched off the ground, Moss wanted to jump out but he tried to remain calm and listen to Neil.

"I took the job knowing full well that there probably was no upward mobility. These kinds of jobs attract lifers, you know? Well, can you believe it, my boss got sick just a few years after I joined up. I have to admit, I felt a little underqualified when I got the promotion, but I knew I was still the best applicant.

"I'll tell ya, I don't think I've ever seen my wife happier than when I called her up that day and told her I got the raise. I think it was even better than the birth of our kid, but she never really took to motherhood, if I'm being honest. I think she really did it because it was the thing to do, you know? All our friends were having kids and it was *that* time in our lives. But really, she never got that into it.

"I was really the primary parent," he continued. Moss clutched the rusted handrail, his grip so tight that he could feel the ancient paint beneath his hand begin to crack and chip. The city got smaller and smaller, and Moss knew he should look away from the ground but couldn't stop staring.

The surrounding casinos were alive with activity. The hotels on top of them all had rooftop pools, gardens and bars, which shrank away as they moved.

Moss could hardly feel his legs when the box jolted to a stop. The air was cold and whipped around them at this height. Neil laughed, looking at Moss.

"Want me to tell you to calm down?" he joked, and Moss wanted to punch him though he did not have the strength. He was just concentrating on putting one foot in front of the other.

Judy just looked at him with wide eyes.

"I have a thing with heights," Moss forced from his mouth.

Neil let out a large stage laugh at that. "Yeah, a thing called fear."

"Shut up," Judy and Moss said in unison. Moss wasn't sure if he preferred this Neil or the previous shitty version.

"You two need to unwind," Neil said. "You ever play craps?"

Judy pushed him out of the elevator and onto the narrow metal catwalk.

"My office is just up here," he said. "We can catch the elevator to the top from there."

"Another level?" Moss asked, his voice shaking.

Neil turned back, his hair whipping in the wind. He looked at Judy. "This kid for real?"

That was all Moss needed to hear. He wouldn't let some junkie mock him outright. He took more steps, ignoring the height and thinking about what they were trying to accomplish. Speaking with the colonies would be the game-changer they needed. He had been frustrated with the way things were going and always feeling like they were on the run. This would change things.

His knuckles were white as he moved; every clanging step shook. But he did it.

Eventually, mercifully, they reached the door to the office. The metal structure jutted out, with big, wired safety glass windows looking down onto the city. Neil shifted his weight to lean over the railing and look into the office.

"Shit," he said quietly, the nerves creeping back in. "Of course it's fucking Rita."

Moss just wanted to get inside and hated the delay. The metal groaned and shifted under his weight and he felt his stomach knot.

"Who's Rita?" Judy hissed.

Neil shook his head, sweat beginning to bead again. "One of those nosy know-it-all types," he said a whiny, deflated voice. "She's going to press me and make me tell her who you are. And I know that cousin line isn't going to fly."

"You're the boss. Can't you just ignore her questions?" Judy suggested.

"Not without raising suspicion and she loves to go to my supervisor," he groused. He and Judy stood quietly a moment, both considering their options.

Moss wanted off this catwalk.

He wanted off this building.

He wanted to be done with this mission.

He wanted some time to rest up and hang out with Issy.

His body began to move.

He pushed passed Neil and Judy, snatching Neil's ID badge off his elastic waistband and swiping it. The door beeped and Rita looked up from her workstation of a few screens set into a large metal control panel, her eyes in complete shock to see a stranger walk in.

He flipped his Kingfisher to non-lethal as he pulled it and she didn't even have time to react before her body was convulsing on the floor. Cold air whistled into the office as Moss turned to see Neil and Judy looking as surprised as Rita had.

"No, no, no," Neil complained.

Moss's body was still shaking slightly with fear but his mind was clear. "We are paying you a small fortune," he reminded the terrified man. "You won't need this job a half hour from now."

"Okay," he said in a tremulous voice. "It's just, I'm all my kid has after my wife left us."

Judy groaned in judgement but didn't say anything. Neil stood frozen, looking at Rita lying on the ground.

"Come in off that catwalk before I throw you off it." Moss's words sounded like his grandmother's. Neil nodded and stepped in, pointing to an open door at the rear of the office leading up more metal stairs.

"We have to hurry," Neil told them, frantic once again. "She has a call with her partner every break on the dot and," he looked at the clock set into the control panel, "we only have a few minutes. Rita doesn't make the call. Her partner is going to think something is really wrong."

"Shit," Moss said, looking at the body on the floor.

"We gotta go," Judy said and began to hustle through the door.

They ascended through a tight metal tube, sporadically lit with afterthought fixtures. Moss's breaths came in ragged jolts as they stepped out of the door to a small platform with an even smaller elevator leading to the top of the tower.

"This is it," Neil said but his mind was clearly still down the stairs.

He pulled a large control switch dangling on thick wires and called the elevator. The sounds it made as it squealed down to them were more terrifying to Moss than a gunshot. It stopped and Moss felt Judy's hand on his back, gently nudging him in.

"We are just about done here," they said.

He chuckled nervously. "At least we aren't surrounded."

Judy knocked a fist against their head superstitiously.

Neil closed them in and once again, they lifted.

Once again, Moss wished he was anywhere else.

He perceived the air getting thinner but he wasn't sure if it was real or in his head. Neil opened the door and pointed down another narrow catwalk. Moss tried not to look down, noticing that even the flighted traffic was below them. Red lights flashed above their heads, reflecting on the shifting fog. The tower lay to the left with dishes and control boxes affixed all over. To the right there was nothing; just a long drop.

"This way," Neil said loudly to make himself heard over the shifting air.

They followed as he guided them to a large metal box surrounded by smaller metal boxes attached to the tower. Thick cables cased in metal tubing snaked out from the back.

Judy set down the case, pulling out a multitool and flipping it open to begin turning the screws on the faceplate.

Neil laughed. "Little trick," he said, manually turning the top rightmost screw twice with his finger and thumb before pulling the plate off. "It's always dummy locked. Techs don't like to waste time."

Judy grinned. "We used to do something similar at the shop." They looked back down, pulling a long cord from the case they had brought and jacking it into the control panel.

Anders, you ready? they communicated.

Moss waited nervously as the cold air shifted around him. He clenched his teeth against the cold and turned, knowing he shouldn't. They were so far off the ground. He swallowed, realizing how dry his mouth was.

Ready, Anders affirmed.

Moss was tense but he also couldn't help but think about how huge this was. They were on the precipice of something remarkable. If this worked, if they could communicate with the off-worlders, they might actually stand a chance down here. He had been assuring himself and the team they would no longer be eternally on the defensive and now, with this, it might actually be true.

Judy gestured for Neil to get to work. He squeezed over to the panel and began to type commands on the small, raised plastic keyboard. Judy tinkered with something in the box as he worked.

"What's this?" he asked to himself.

"What?" Judy asked.

The nervousness was obvious in their words.

"Hold on," he said. "Oh, man, this has some advanced tech. This system is new and needs a firmware update."

"Shit," Judy said.

"I'm going to have to run back down to the office and run the patch from there," Neil told them. "But you should know that I do have keystroke accountability in place, so it may raise some alarms."

"Shit!" Judy said again.

They had come so far just to be stymied by a small problem like this.

"Cheat code?" Moss asked and saw Judy close their eyes in defeat.

"Cheat code."

Moss sat on the walkway. The little raised metal circles meant to grip boots dug into his flesh. He looked at Judy. "Please," he began but they smiled and held up a hand.

"I won't let you fall," they said.

"Aww, touching," Neil interjected.

"I swear . . . " Judy began to threaten but Moss closed his eyes and the world dropped away.

His hex once more.

He stood first, as he always did, and began to walk to his workstation. He cocked his head as he noticed one of the fluorescent bulbs overhead begin to flicker.

It made his heart stop. This was a program. It was not meant to do that. Was it his own mind? Was his unconscious trying to tell him something?

He stared into the bulb and it flickered again. He walked closer to examine it through the plastic cover.

He turned his head, saying aloud, "I don't have time for this."

Even if it was a warning or a glitch, he had something he needed to do. He remembered Neil's warning about Rita and knew he should move quickly, in the heat of the moment forgetting that time had slowed to a crawl.

He accessed the computer and brought up the local systems. They weren't hard to find. Everything was clearly labeled and he was happy that CommiTech made things so obvious. He scrolled down and found the update. When he selected it, an error message appeared.

NETWORK CONNECTION REQUIRED

Moss's shoulders fell.

He tried again and got the same message.

He opened the dropdown for local networks and saw CMTechTWR13.

He connected to the network. The download started instantly, the bar beginning to fill.

"What *are* you doing?" Arthur Smith's voice asked.

Moss turned to see the man standing in his hex, wearing a finely-pinstriped blue business suit. Moss felt his fists ball.

"What are you?" Moss asked.

"Why," the man said, sweeping his arms wide. "I'm Arthur Smith, president of ThutoCo and your employer."

He grinned and Moss moved toward him.

"Are you a creation of my mind?"

Arthur shrugged. "I am *in* your mind."

Moss grabbed him by the collar and Arthur didn't fight it. He just continued to grin.

"What are you?" Moss said again, louder this time, pushing the man up against the wall.

He just kept smiling.

"What are you?" Moss shrieked and moved to punch the man. Moss's fist moved slowly as if underwater, and when it struck Arthur's face, it landed lightly with a dull thud.

He laughed. Moss felt rage.

Arthur looked over Moss's shoulder. His eyes went wide with delight. "CommiTech," he observed and looked away from Moss a moment.

Moss turned to see that the download was only at thirty percent.

"You're using the Carcer technology?" Arthur said in astonishment. Moss moved to try and punch him again, but the man vanished into a digital void. Moss turned, looking around his empty hex before hearing another familiar voice.

"We will get our tech back and you will die," Warden Ninety-Nine said.

Seeing him actually put Moss at ease. He had feared Arthur was a hack but knew that Ninety-Nine had to be a figment of his own mind.

"Why I put you in here, I will never know," Moss told the man, almost absentmindedly. It worried him that his mind was playing these kinds of tricks on him, but he almost didn't care; he was just so happy that it was *his* mind.

His body lurched within the program.

"The fuck?"

It moved again and this time he fell to the ground.

Eighty-eight percent.

He was nervous now. Something was wrong. A lot of things were wrong.

A call box appeared on his screen. He got to his feet and accepted the call.

He heard Judy's frantic voice yelling, "What's going on in there? You're screaming."

He could hear his own shouts in the background, the screams of someone who can't hear his own voice.

The program was breaking, his mind was breaking. While it was good that they were no longer hacking him, his own brain was hacking itself.

Ninety-four percent.

"You are going to make this too easy on us," the warden said with a wide grin, putting his armored boot up on one of the arms of the couch.

Moss needed to get out of here. He waited and saw it reach one hundred percent.

He ran over and began to install the update.

Looking at the warden one last time, he closed his eyes in the program, willing himself back into the world. Rather than the hex fading away, it began to melt and stretch. He had the sensation of falling as he was pulled through the air.

His body began to spin and twirl as he fell.

"Judy?" he called but there was no answer. The connection had been severed, if it was ever real.

He smelled vomit.

He reached out to try and grab the wall, pull at something.

Nothing worked. The wall receded away from his touch.

He fell faster.

He should never have done this.

He closed his eyes again and focused.

The movement made it difficult. He tried to pull his own mind back into his control.

He thought about what they were doing, how close they were.

Things were about to change, but he needed to survive this.

"Moss!" he heard Issy say. The voice, her voice was what he needed.

He felt himself breathe. The world slowed. He focused on her voice.

"Moss," she said again and he grabbed at it, reaching out with the tendrils of his mind.

"Issy," he said, his words hardening rather than vaporizing into the void.

He saw black. He felt cloth against his face, wiping it. He sputtered, realizing he was on his side. He looked out over the city, gasping for air. His throat burned. Judy's hands were on his back and shoulders, keeping him in place.

"Establish a connection now," Judy ordered Neil.

"On it," Moss heard before the clanking of boots behind him. The metal rattled and shook, and Moss reached out to grip the base of the railing. Pulling himself up, he watched as Neil booted the system.

"You're in," he said with a laugh of relief. "I almost can't believe it."

Moss felt fear in the pit of his stomach. This is when things always went wrong. Carcer or ThutoCo would show up and the firefight would ensue. He looked over the ledge.

Nothing.

Just the city. Massive megabuildings enthroned atop layers of low poverty.

Flighted cars moved in their perfect patterns and the wind cried, but nothing else.

Got the link, Anders informed them. *Get out of there.*

Moss sighed, just before an alarm blared.

"There it is," Moss grinned miserably. From the base of the tower, drones began to fire up , lifting rapidly into the air towards them.

Judy yanked the connection and shut the box with the stolen equipment before setting up another overcooker. Pulling off their jacket, Judy exposed their dronepack, quickly preparing for a flying escape. They hustled over to Moss, pulling him up.

Neil looked at them with an odd confidence. "I'll go back down to the office. Say you knocked me out too."

"You sure they won't suspect you?" Moss asked, the smell of his own mouth nauseating him.

"They might but I have a better chance trying to sell them a lie," he said. "I disappear now, they'll know it was me. My life will be ruined. My child's life will be ruined. I have to at least try."

"Good luck to you," Moss said, pulling the cash chip out of his pocket with an unsteady hand. "Thank you."

As Neil took the chip, turning it over in his hand, Judy moved past them. They hustled quickly to the stairs and began setting a charge. They needed time before CommiTech and Carcer came to solve the problem.

Judy finished prepping the explosive and produced a detonator before standing and hurrying over. "Better make yourself scarce," they said, but Neil was too focused on the chip to notice. Moss figured the man was dreaming of all the ways he could gamble away the money they had given him, but when he looked up, his eyes were wet.

"Thank you both," he croaked, his voice breaking with genuine gratitude. "This will be my new beginning," he said and slid the chip cap open to expose the digital display and find out how much they were paying him.

His eyebrows furrowed at all the zeros and the chip popped loudly. He dropped it and looked up at Moss in confusion. He blinked and Moss noticed crimson liquid. First a drop from the corner of one eye, then the other and finally, his mouth and nose.

Moss and Judy watched in horror as he gripped the railing and turned to look out. "Pat," he miserably sputtered his child's name one final time, blood pouring down his body before he keeled over and plummeted.

"What?" Moss said, the sounds of the drones drowned out by his own heartbeat in his ears.

"Fucking Sandra," Judy snarled. "We have to go," they ordered Moss, stepping behind him and pulling off his coat.

Moss was numb. He hadn't particularly liked the man, but he certainly hadn't deserved to die. He had helped them, gotten them here and his thanks was an early grave. He knew his grandmother would say she was just covering their tracks, not leaving any loose ends. But he also knew the truth: this man was, even if just in a small way, helping Carcer extend its reach and Sandra wouldn't abide that. The years of confinement and torture at the company's hands had damaged her too much to allow anyone who worked with them to live.

Judy grabbed the sides of his face.

His mind was swimming.

The success.

The death.

The program.

All of it.

"We. Have. To. Go!" they repeated and pressed the button on his chest to start the dronepack. Moss felt the thrusters start and his feet lift off the metal.

The drones began to buzz toward them, locking on and pointing weapons.

Judy fired their EMP Rifle, knocking drone after drone from the sky as they flew away. They pressed the detonator and the air vibrated with the explosion from the tower, the only passage to the communication array temporarily destroyed — until the company got techs with their own dronepacks.

More security drones closed in, beginning to get near enough to fire precise shots. Judy blasted one, then another, but the swarm moved in.

"Moss!" they screamed as small red lights on the drones flared on and the guns swiveled to face them.

He stared into the barrels of his death. He would be shot from the sky and fall so far that his remains would have to be genetically identified.

"Moss!" Judy shouted again, sending more bolts through the sky.

He clenched his jaw and looked right at one of the drones. "Fuck this," he said and grabbed his mind. He took control of himself in a way he never had before. He felt the program but didn't dip into it.

He pulled it toward him.

He moved it forward and out.

He watched the closest drone turn at his will. Its muzzle flashed in the night as bullet-shell rain fell. The drone in his control blasted the others to bits, sending chunks of flaming metal hurtling down. The other drones' programs tried to assess what to do, but not in time.

Judy's mouth fell open as they looked at Moss's wide eyes, sensing his mind controlling the machine.

When the puppet drone was all that remained, Moss felt his eye twitch. The gun protruding from the base of the circular robot pointed upward at its own chassis, shredding itself and falling away with a trail of smoke.

Moss thought he heard a cackle before the sound of his dronepack was all that remained. They glided quietly between massive buildings for a moment, as Moss felt his eyelids getting heavy.

He had done something he had never thought possible. Something he had not even considered.

The program was broken and poisoning his mind. It was now also the most powerful weapon at their disposal. The sharpest double-edged sword on Earth.

"Moss," Judy said, looking over their shoulder with worry written on their face.

He blinked slowly, deeply.

Then he heard in his mind's ear, "Captain Amakum?" in a woman's voice he did not recognize.

"It's me," Anders said.

"How the hell are you?" the voice asked from somewhere out in space. "Last I heard you were heading back to Earth after-"

Anders cut in. "I'm here now and need your help. We want to work with the colonies. The Carcer Corporation is looking to expand your way and we want to stop that."

Moss felt his eyes close, the city fading to black.

"We have some conditions," the woman's voice said. "But if you want to fix Earth, we'll help."

Before dropping into the void, Moss smiled.

THE END

EPILOGUE

Arthur Smith sighed. The long, slow breath was the physical embodiment of everything he was feeling. The CEO of ThutoCo had been so close. He thought he had Moss's mind well in hand. He had laid the perfect trap, pulled out all the stops and had once again been defeated. This small crew of terrorists was making the largest companies in the world look like amateurs.

He sighed again, lifting the glass of seventy-year aged pinotage. The deep purple color reflected the light streaking in from his window in a shimmering dance as the wine caught the fading yellow. This blend was one of the few things that still connected him to his home country.

He had not been back for ages, not since his wife had taken the kids and gone home. He gazed at the digital picture on his desk. It had not been changed in several years; his daughters looked so different now. When he made it to their weekly call, they no longer resembled the sweet little girls frozen in time on his desk.

He wished he could see them more. Wished his job allowed him more free time. Wished that bitch of a wife hadn't taken them from him.

He took another sip, letting the wine coat his mouth before swallowing.

Shaking his head, he stood up, wishing he did not have to speak with the Amalgamated Interests Council anymore. Things were tense now. Everyone blamed him for these rebels that were causing so many problems. They all looked to him to destroy them and every time he tried, he failed.

He felt his jaw clench as he thought about Moss.

He hated that kid with a burning rage. Hated the AIC for blaming him. Hated that warden who was undoubtedly about to bust his balls. Hated his employees who kept making mistakes and letting these people continue to slip through their grasp.

He hated them all. He tried to take a calming breath but fury took over and he sent the glass of wine hurtling across the room to smash against a bookshelf.

This office had remained unchanged since ThutoCo's founder had died generations ago. Wesley Grayson had stipulated in his will that all new CEOs should find the time to read the works he had carefully assembled on the shelf. Arthur didn't know if the others before him had read any, but he had not.

Any free time he had would be much better spent with a relief aide than a book.

The wine dribbled slowly down the books, devaluing them more than the salaries of an entire burb's worth of employees combined.

A chime rang out before his automated assistant said, "The mayor is here to see you."

Arthur groaned before falling back into his leather chair. He rubbed his hands over his face. This was the last thing he wanted to deal with before his meeting. The mayor's term was coming to a close and Arthur was sure that Duke Doland Junior was here to ask for money to get whatever child or lackey he desired elected.

Arthur despised the mayor's office. It was nothing but a relic of another time — a time when governments had actual authority. Now it was little more than a ceremonial position with almost no power and which made no decisions without the express consent of the AIC.

"Let him in," Arthur sighed, wishing the man had simply called rather than showing up at his office.

The office itself was beautiful and had been designed by one of the most famous architects at the time of construction. Arthur didn't care for it, finding the simple and sleek design uninteresting. To make the space more exciting, he had knocked out part of the wall to the right of his desk opposite the bookshelf and filled it with a taxidermied shark he had killed. The massive gray beast had eluded him for a week when on a trip off the coast of the city, but Arthur had finally nailed it. On a choppy, hazy morning, the big fish had neared the surface enough for Arthur to shoot it.

There were few left on Earth, and it had given Arthur so much pleasure to end the life of the creature said to be one of the planet's best hunters. Even looking at it now made him happy.

The door to the office hissed open and Mayor Doland stepped in. He wore a fine expertly-tailored suit and the smartshades he had become famous for always wearing. His graying hair was coiffed with an unnatural microdye shimmer. He wore a serious expression on his artificially tanned face.

Arthur grimaced as a second figure shadowed the door.

Warden Ninety-Nine strode in wearing his full black armor with red trim. He sneered at Arthur as he strode forward, pulling one booted foot up on a low chair. The temporary head of the Carcer Corporation had made his dislike of Arthur clear on every single occasion and Arthur returned the sentiment.

"Mister Smith," Duke said, flashing teeth so white as to be blinding.

"Mister Mayor," Arthur said, before acknowledging, "Warden."

There was a tense silence.

"What can I do for you gentlemen?" Arthur asked, all false kindness.

"Um," Duke said uncomfortably, pulling at a cufflink. "The city has reached an agreement with Carcer Corp."

Arthur felt his stomach knot. There was no good version of this. No matter what it was, Carcer was about to become more powerful and a sharper thorn in the side of ThutoCo.

Arthur wished he didn't need the other companies to see his plans through. He wished he could do away with all these so-called allies who would smile to your face while stabbing you in the back.

He swore to himself that as soon as he had accomplished his goals, he would do away with all these phony partners. Until that day, he would have to suffer them.

He smiled. "What's that?" He was an expert liar and his voice did not betray his thoughts, though the two men before him undoubtedly knew what he was thinking.

"I was approached by the Carcer Corporation after your employee's attack on CommiTech Tower."

Arthur held up a hand, feeling the blood rush to his face. "Former employee! You say it as though he was on his lunch break. This terrorist no longer works for me and I am not responsible for his actions.”

Warden Ninety-Nine seemed amused by the outburst, smirking and running his thumb and forefinger slowly down his moustache. “Moss may not work for you, but you raised him, made him what he is. The program in his mind was constructed at ThutoCo and you are the reason he has a vendetta.

“You can try and pass the blame as much as you want, but we both know he is your doing and, if you are not careful, your undoing.

“You have this whole plan, all these wheels in motion, but this kid who ‘doesn’t work for you’ may ruin everything,” Ninety-Nine said.

Arthur felt his fist clench. He hated Warden Ninety-Nine most of all, maybe even more than Moss. The smug asshole made his blood boil, and all the worse because he was right.

Duke cleared his throat. “That aside, we have decided it is time to rid the city of these rebels. They are getting too bold and their numbers are increasing. I will announce this afternoon that, until further notice, B.A. City is under martial law. Carcer will take full control of the streets and keep our companies safe until these people are dealt with.”

Arthur felt his mouth fall open and then he laughed. It was a pure, unadulterated laugh that came from deep within him.

“You fools,” he sneered. “The people are getting angrier and your solution is a boot on their necks. This plan will give them more strength, more influence. They will see you for what you are: power-hungry weaklings scared of the collective will of the people. You will appear to be grasping at power rather than asserting it.

"You don't have nearly the manpower needed to control this city. It will be a claim and little more. Nothing on the streets will change except the people will hate you. This plan will be your undoing, both of you."

He couldn't stop shaking his head.

The two men who stood before him looked at Arthur as if he was the fool and he returned the exact look.

"We knew you would be upset," Duke observed.

"Perhaps it is because he really *does* want Moss to succeed," Ninety-Nine said to the mayor.

Arthur stood angrily, his chair tumbling backwards with the force of the movement.

"Do what you have to do. Lock down the city and drive the people into the waiting arms of the terrorists," Arthur said in exasperation.

"We are all on the same team," Duke offered.

"Right," Arthur said miserably. It had been true. Once.

When he had brought the heads of the major companies together, he had wanted it to be a partnership that benefited them all and for years it had. But he had been naïve. He had fooled himself into believing that people at the top of their respective fields could come together and stay united.

The infighting had started quickly and he knew that the Council would already have fallen to ruins had Arthur not been driving them toward the goal that would ensure a wealthier future. Alice Carcer had seen the benefit too and worked the group to her advantage, but Warden Ninety-Nine was a different animal.

He wanted power, direct control, rather than the puppeteer influence of the AIC.

And he was getting it.

Arthur couldn't help but ask himself if things were better now than they had been with Alice. When she was alive, they had duked it out, but there was a mutual respect. With Ninety-Nine, it was pure loathing.

"Was there anything else?"

Warden Ninety-Nine and the mayor shared a look. "No," Duke said.

The warden smiled. "I will see you at the meeting after our announcement."

"Fine," Arthur sighed.

"Rest assured," Ninety-Nine said, standing. His imposing frame loomed ominously in the fading light of the day. "Once we secure the city, we *will* find Moss and destroy him."

Arthur exhaled, looking with pity at the two people standing before him.

"Okay," he said finally. He was tired. Tired of the same old threats, tired of the same repeated claims. He was done with it all.

These idiots would lock down the city and find themselves in a new world of pain. Meanwhile, Arthur would do the real work of tracking down Moss while Carcer fought with every pissant citizen on the street.

He smiled at the thought.

He would take down Moss, utilize that program in his head and finally move forward with his plan.

He looked up at Ninety-Nine and the mayor with a serene look on his face.

"You can get out of my office now."

NOTE TO THE READER

Thanks for reading *Into Neon: A Cyberpunk Saga.* If you enjoyed the book, please leave a review; it is incredibly helpful to new authors. Reviews are one of the ways in which people can discover new work and help me to create more of it. Thanks again for reading.

For free content, a glossary of terms, cosplay, concept art and much more, visit Thutoworld.com

AUTHOR BIO

Matthew A. Goodwin has been writing about spaceships, dragons, and adventures since he was twelve years old. His passion for fantasy began when he discovered a box set of the Hobbit radio drama on cassette tape in his school's library at the age of seven. He fell in love with fantasy worlds and soon discovered D&D and Warhammer miniatures.

Not wanting to be limited by worlds designed by others, he created Thutopia (now called the Thuton Empire), a fantasy world of his own, which he still writes about to this day.

Like many kids with an affinity for fantasy, a love of science fiction soon followed. He loved sweeping space operas and gritty cyberpunk stories which asked questions about man's relationship to technology. That led him to write his first published work, *Into Neon: A Cyberpunk Saga*, which takes place in a larger science fiction universe.

He has a passion for travel and wildlife, and when he is not off trying to see the world, he lives in San Francisco with his wife and son.